The Unusual Ministries of Father Kein Laimend

Book 2

The Silence of Saints

Written by: Marcus Bebee

The Unusual Ministries of Father Kein Laimend

Book Two: The Silence of Saints

ISBN: 979-8-9945608-2-2

Published by Marcus Bebee

First Edition, 2026.

Printed in the United States of America.

Published by Marcus Bebee

First Edition, 2026.

Printed in the United States of America.

Dedication

This book is once again dedicated to the same three people.

First, to my beautiful wife, Morgan. You are the reason *The Unusual Ministries* were ever born. Your love, patience, and quiet faith carried these stories from their first uncertain pages to life. Thank you for reading every draft, for gently guiding me when I lost my way, and for trusting Darby to continue her journey alongside Father Kein. Your presence is a constant grace in my life, and everything I write is touched by it. I love you.

Second, to our good friend Ashley. Thank you again for allowing Rozas to be Kein's voice of reason when his is failing and for continuing on the journey with him. Your personality resonates through Rozas on the pages, at least in my mind it does, and he is pretty hard core so...

And finally, to Father Keith, the inspiration for the character of Father Kein Laimend. Your weekly words of faith, hope and God are more meaningful to those of us that sit in the pews than you could imagine. You are an inspiration to us all to be better people. We appreciate you so much.

Author's Note

This second book arrived unexpectedly, much like the first. Once I began writing, the words poured onto the page in a rush—less like careful construction and more like a fire hose, impossible to stop once it began. I followed along with the story as it revealed itself, and I was on the edge of my seat as much as I hope you will be. When I finished the last page, I sat back and was astonished at what had just transpired.

I did not outline this story or plan its course. I trusted it to lead where it needed to go, even when that path felt uncertain or unsettling. What emerged surprised me, challenged me and drew me even closer to the characters who now feel very real to me.

Thank you for continuing this journey with us.

Father Kein's story is far from over, but in his words, "All in God's timing."

Prologue

Book Two: The Silence of Saints

The church opened on schedule.

Lights were already on. Candles burned in straight lines along the altar. The air was still. Parishioners entered and took their places without speaking, filling the pews in the same pattern as always.

Footsteps passed through the aisles and did not linger. Hymnals were set flush with the wood. Statues stood clean and unmarked. Nothing was out of place.

When the bells rang, the sound echoed through the building and faded.

Inside, the silence remained unchanged.

Introduction

Father Kein Laimend (pronounced Keen Lay Mon) is a priest shaped by a past few would willingly carry. Haunted by loss, faith, and unanswered questions, he has learned that ministry is rarely about certainty and never about comfort. His calling has led him into places where belief is tested quietly and obedience carries an unseen cost.

His new assignment appears peaceful—an ordered parish, a devoted congregation, and a Cathedral that stands as a symbol of stability. Yet beneath its beauty and routine, something watches and waits, hiding not in chaos but in familiarity.

This is a story about the danger of quiet evil and the weight of discernment when God's voice seems distant. It is about learning that silence is not always absence—and that faith must sometimes stand alone, without reassurance.

The Unusual Ministries of Father Kein Laimend

Book 2

The Silence of Saints

Written by: Marcus Bebee

Contents

Chapter 1

A New Calling

Father Kein opened his eyes.

He was in a hospital bed. Wires and steady beeping surrounded him. The smell of antiseptic hung in the air—unmistakable. He remembered walking back to his church. He remembered seeing Joseph and Sandy. Were they real? The letter—his transfer letter. He never opened it.

He remembered everything going dark. The sound of his head hitting the porch.

Then nothing.

When was that? How long had it been?

Kein reached up and gently touched his head where it had struck the floor. Still painful. *Can't have been too long if it still hurts this bad,* he thought.
"Still painful," he muttered aloud through a dry throat.

His voice stirred the room.

Someone was there—sleeping on a makeshift bed against the wall.

"Father... you're awake," a male voice whispered. "How do you feel?"

Kein squinted, his vision still blurry. "I feel... well, I'm not sure exactly. Where am I?"

"You're in the hospital. Darby found you on the porch of Our Lady. You fell and hit your head pretty bad."

The voice sounded familiar. "Rozas? Is that you?" Kein asked.

"Yes, my friend. It is me. I came as soon as the hospital called." Rozas stepped closer.

Kein remembered adding Rozas as his emergency contact. "How long has it been, Rozas?"

"Twelve days, Kein. You've been unconscious the entire time. The doctors will want to talk to you. Let me get the nurse."

"What time is it?" Kein asked.

"It's two in the morning. Why?"

"Let me just get my bearings first, please."

Rozas was already moving toward the door. "No. They'll need to check your vitals, then you can rest."

The door closed behind him. Kein heard his voice echoing down the hallway.
"Nurse! Nurse... Father Laimend woke up. We need someone in here."

Kein closed his eyes as his head began to throb.

The door opened again. He forced his eyes open and saw Rozas more clearly now. He had allowed his beard to grow, it was unkempt, gray beginning to show. *Has he been here the whole time?*

"Father Kein, how are you feeling?" a woman asked. "I'm Nurse Kim. Can you open your eyes wide for me?"

Before he could answer, she examined him, shining a small flashlight into his eyes.

“That’s good,” she said, tapping buttons on a nearby monitor. “Everything looks stable. How are you feeling?”

“I’m fine. My head hurts where I fell, but otherwise I’m fine.”

“That’s encouraging. Do you remember falling? What’s the last thing you remember?”

“I remember stopping by for some Tylenol. I had a headache. Then I checked my mail… and that’s about it.”

She nodded. “That lines up with what we were told.” She adjusted his IV. “I’m going to give you something to help you rest. We’ll talk more in the morning.”

She injected a clear liquid into the IV line. The room began to tilt gently. As his eyes closed, Kein heard Rozas speaking softly.

“This is a good sign, right?”

“Possibly,” the nurse replied. “The doctor will explain more in the morning.”

When Kein opened his eyes again, sunlight streamed through the curtains. Voices and footsteps filled the hallway. Life moved on around him.

The clock on the wall read 2:15.

He had slept away most of the day.

The room was empty. Rozas must have gone out—perhaps to get lunch. Kein pressed the red call button.

Moments later, Nurse Kim returned. “Good afternoon, Father. How are you feeling today?”

Same nurse. She must have the late shift “Better, thank you. How long will I need to stay?”

“The doctor will be in shortly. You can discuss that with her.” She checked the monitors. “Everything looks normal. I’ll let her know you’re awake.”

A short time later, a young woman entered. She had black hair and appeared to be of Asian descent.

“Hello, Father Kein. I’m Doctor Young. I’ve been overseeing your care. How are you feeling?”

“Much better. When can I leave? I have a lot to catch up on—and I’m hungry.”

“Well, you were unconscious for twelve days, so we need to talk about what’s going on.”

At that moment, Rozas returned. “Ah, Kein. You’re awake. Doctor, how is he?”

“He’s stable. Vitals are good. But we need to discuss his condition.”

“Condition?” Kein frowned. “I just got dizzy and fell.”

“We thought that at first,” Doctor Young said. “Have you had dizziness before? Headaches? Tunnel vision?”

“I’ve been under stress lately, but yes—headaches. Nothing unusual, I thought.”

Rozas spoke carefully. “Kein, while you were unconscious, I went to Williamstown. I spoke with John at the pharmacy. He said you’ve been using quite a bit of medication.”

Doctor Young continued, “We ran several tests. You have a small meningioma—a benign tumor in the meninges, the protective layer around the brain. It isn’t cancerous, but its location is concerning. It’s pressing on your frontal lobe, which explains the headaches and likely caused your blackout.”

“I see,” Kein said quietly. “What does this mean?”

“Surgery is risky due to the location. The frontal lobes control cognition. Removing it now could cause more harm than good. Our recommendation is radiation therapy to shrink it first.”

“And if I choose not to?”

“Then the tumor may grow, leading to loss of motor control, worsening headaches, and possible blackouts.”

“In other words,” Kein said calmly, “I become a burden either way.”

“Well—” Doctor Young began.

“I appreciate the care you’ve given me,” Kein interrupted. “But I’ll be fine. When can I be discharged?”

“Kein—” Rozas started.

“No,” Kein said firmly. “We’ll discuss this later. Please.”

“Well, technically you are fine. All of your tests look good otherwise, and you can go home whenever you like,” Dr. Young said.

"Very well, then I'd like to—"

Rozas cut in. "He will stay one more night for observation. Thank you, Doctor."

Dr. Young nodded and walked out of the room.

"Rozas, I don't need to stay here. I'm fine," Kein said.

"You will," Rozas replied firmly, "or I will submit a recommendation to have you assessed for medical retirement, my friend."

Rozas was serious.

"Fine. I will stay the night. Tell me, how is Our Lady Queen of Prayer?" Kein asked.

"It is wonderful. You brought life back to that place—the breath of God into those people. Father Jeremy is covering your absence until it is relinquished to Father Monroe. I know you're being transferred, my friend." Rozas walked to the cabinet and retrieved a yellow envelope. "I have your mail from the porch."

He handed it to Kein and smiled. "You are more than deserving of a wonderful church and congregation."

"Yes, that would be nice, Rozas," Kein said as he accepted the envelope.

Rozas stepped out to give him privacy.

Kein opened the envelope and removed a letter and a key. He began to read:

To:
Father Kein Laimend,

We hope this letter finds you in good health and continued blessings. We are writing to inform you of a new assignment, effective December 1, two thousand twenty-six.

Father Laimend reassignment schedule as follows:

Relinquish leadership of Our Lady Queen of Prayer, Williamstown, Texas, to Father Kevin Monroe.
Assume leadership of Saint Augustine's Holy Cathedral, Redmond, North Carolina.

God's service through you is always appreciated.

Blessed be,
Bishop Andrew Miller

"A cathedral," Kein said quietly to himself. "What an honor. And Saint Augustine of Hippo—what a great namesake."

He called Rozas back in to share the news. They spent the rest of the afternoon talking about the cathedral and what the assignment meant. They spoke of the sadness of leaving Williamstown, then rejoiced over all that had happened there—the good that had come through faith and service. The joy of it all overshadowed the reality of the tumor and what it meant for Kein.

The next day, Kein dressed and was released from the hospital. Dr. Young once again urged him to consider radiation treatment, which he declined, thanking her for her concern.

"I'm going to have to recommend that your driver's license be suspended," she said. "You're a hazard behind the wheel with this condition. If you were to blackout and cause an accident, I couldn't live with that."

Kein stopped and turned back. "What? You don't need to—"

"Yes, I do, Father," she interrupted. "I submitted the paperwork this morning. You are not well, and I don't want this to lead to a greater tragedy. No pun intended."

Kein paused, then composed himself. He turned to face her. At 5'9", he stood level with the woman. "I understand, Doctor. I appreciate your concern. I will pray for guidance. Thank you."

With that, he left the hospital and met Rozas at the curb.

"My friend, you need to reconsider the treatment," Rozas said as they drove back toward Williamstown.

"I can't risk losing the ability to give Mass—or even to care for myself," Kein replied. "It's not something I'm willing to entertain right now. I'll have my car shipped to North Carolina and leave it parked until I figure things out."

"I will pray for you, Kein. I know God has great plans for you, and I'm grateful to have been part of your journey," Rozas said.

The following week was spent packing and saying goodbye to the town that had become his family. Kein ate at the 432 Café and spent time with Darby. He gave Scott instructions until the new priest arrived. He tied up loose ends, mailed his black credit card to the archdiocese and arranged for his car to be shipped.

Saying goodbye was never easy.

He cleaned the church—the one Joseph had repaired. He truly believed Saint Joseph, Jesus's earthly father, had helped restore it. That night, he sat alone in the pews and wept softly before going to sleep.

The next morning, his ride to the airport waited outside. He picked a satsuma from the tree he had planted and climbed into the car.

The airport had never been his favorite place. He remembered the words spoken by the demon years ago: *You will die, falling from the air and wishing you had a diaper, Priest Kein.* A chill ran through him. He would forever hear that voice—spoken through a young girl. Flying unsettled him because of it.

At the airport, Kein unloaded his bags, tipped the driver, and made his way to the gate. He was hopeful. He had never been to North Carolina, and the assignment felt like a fresh beginning.

Once seated on the plane, he buckled in and prepared for takeoff. He took headache medicine and tried to relax.

This is going to be a good flight, he told himself.

He closed his eyes and reflected on his life—his past assignments and the joy he had witnessed when people found Christ. Before he realized it, the plane was landing. The jolt of the wheels touching the runway brought him back.

He gathered his bags and met his ride outside. Snow dusted the ground, and the air was cold. He pulled his coat from his bag and slipped it on.

As the car pulled away, Father Kein Laimend looked out the window, ready for what lay ahead.

“Adventure awaits,” he told himself.

Chapter 2

The Cathedral

Arriving at the Cathedral, it was glorious. A beautiful, tall steeple crowned with bells rose above him. The doors were towering and appeared hand-carved—simply gorgeous. Kein took the key from his pocket and unlocked them. They opened without so much as a squeak.

This place is immaculate, Laimend thought.

Inside, he found a masterfully designed entryway: half walls and columns adorned with gold inlays and exquisite carvings of the Blessed Mother and Saint Joseph. Kein smiled at the statue of Joseph and felt—almost foolishly—that he caught a small smirk in return.

Father Kein made his way through the nave, observing the pews and floor. The marble tiles were outlined with brass inlays, gleaming softly. The pews themselves were deep mahogany, wide and inviting—comfortable, he thought. He continued toward the sanctuary, then stopped and turned to take in the choir loft. A white banister wrapped in gold traced its edge, and from the floor he could see the piano—it was enormous. Twin staircases spiraled upward on either side, wide marble steps paired with elegant handrails.

He turned again, bowed before the massive crucifix mounted on the wall and whispered a brief prayer of thanks. Stepping into the sanctuary, he circled the altar, taking it all in. He knelt to pray—but a voice cut through the silence.

"Excuse me—*excuse me!* Who do you think you are? You can't just—"

The voice stopped abruptly as Kein stepped around the altar and saw a woman striding toward the sanctuary. She was short, with brown hair streaked with gray. He guessed she was in her fifties. She froze when she noticed his collar.

"Oh! I'm so sorry, Father. I didn't see your collar at first."

"That's funny," he said gently. "That's usually what everyone notices first."

"My name is Charlene, and I do apologize," she said, her Southern accent slipping through. "I was just making sure nobody was in here who wasn't supposed to be. I've been working in this church a long time. Father Pete asked me to keep an eye on things until you arrived."

"Well, I'm Father Kein Laimend," he replied. "And I appreciate you taking care of things until I got here, Miss Charlene."

"Oh, it's *Mrs.* Charlene—Mrs. Charlene Baker. My husband is Ronald, and we're very prominent members of the parish."

Kein chuckled softly. "Well, *Mrs.* Charlene, I look forward to getting to know you both."

"Oh, you will, Father. We're here all the time."

"Yes, ma'am," Kein said as he lifted his bag and headed toward the Sacristy. "God is a good thing to be devoted to."

"Yes, Father. And we take care of all the yard work outside and clean up inside sometimes too."

Kein stopped and turned. "Well, I truly appreciate that."

Charlene smiled.

"And now, if you don't mind, I'll get better acquainted with my new quarters and unload my belongings."

"Oh, yes, of course, Father. I'll leave you to it."

Father Kein entered the Sacristy and unpacked his bag, placing his vestments in the closet. The door was heavy, with pearl inlay around the handle. The panels were painted white, the wood intricately etched. His desk was massive—far larger than he could ever fully use. The chair was overstuffed, almost indulgently comfortable.

As he sat, a familiar pressure bloomed behind his eyes.

Not now, he thought.

He reached into his pocket, retrieved his bottle of Tylenol, swallowed two tablets and washed them down with the last of his water. When he stood, dizziness washed over him.

“Stood up too fast,” he muttered.

After a moment, the room steadied. He stepped back into the nave, planning to take the rest of his bags to his new home. It was a few miles away, so he pulled out his phone to call an Uber. As he entered the nave, his eyes landed immediately on Charlene—sitting in the front pew, smiling broadly at him.

“Um... did you need something else, Charlene?” he asked.

“No, Father. I just wanted to make sure you were settled. Do you have any questions? Need anything from me?”

“I’m actually calling an Uber to take me to the house,” he said. “So, I suppose we can walk out together and lock up for now.”

“Oh, I can take you. No need to pay for a ride, Father—it’s only a mile and a half. My car’s right out front.”

“Alright. Thank you very much,” Kein said.

As they reached the steps, Kein turned to lock the door—but Charlene already had her key in hand.

"I've got it, Father. Come on, this way."

She led him to a white Cadillac parked at the curb, its paint gleaming, leather interior pristine. The license plate read: *ILUVJC.*

"This is very kind of you," Kein said as they pulled away. "I don't think I've ever ridden in a Cadillac. It's a very smooth ride."

"Well, yes," Charlene replied. "I can't have you riding around with some stranger. And I know you can't drive right now, with your... well, your head thing."

Kein's stomach tightened.

How does she know that?

"Yes—well, I appreciate it," he said.

The drive felt longer than expected. Charlene filled the silence with talk of the local high school team—the Robins—and the town's comings and goings. Who was doing what. Who to watch out for.

Lots of gossip, Kein thought.

They stopped in front of a small but well-kept house. Two-tone gray-blue siding, a green roof. Immaculate.

"It's three bedrooms, two baths," Charlene said proudly. "I picked it myself. When Father Pete was coming, I couldn't have him living in squalor. I furnished it, too—come on, I'll show you."

She reached for his bag.

"Oh—I can get that," Kein said quickly, taking it from her. "Thank you."

She led him onto the porch, producing another set of keys.

"Yes, well, I just had the house washed," she said, unlocking the door. "Isn't it lovely?"

"It is," Kein said carefully. "But I do have my own key."

"Oh, of course. I just thought—come on, I'll show you around. Wipe the slush off your feet there. The fridge is new, and the couch is—"

"Mrs. Charlene," Kein interrupted gently, "I truly appreciate everything you've done. But I'm very tired. It's been a long day. I think I can manage the rest on my own."

Her smile faltered.

"Oh. Yes. Of course, Father."

She moved toward the door, her disappointment evident.

"I don't mean anything by it. I'm truly just very tired from the flight and moving. It'll just take me a bit to get acclimated," Kein said, trying to smooth over the interaction.

"Yes, of course, Father. No problem," Charlene responded and then closed the door.

He felt slightly uncomfortable that she had a key to the Cathedral, but more so that she had a key to his house. She seemed nice enough, though—if a bit overwhelming. Kein took in his surroundings. There was a large couch in front of the TV. He pressed the power button on the remote, and it turned on; there were quite a few channels.

“Ah, it works,” he chuckled to himself.

The kitchen had a small table for dining, and the refrigerator was a two-door stainless-steel behemoth. He opened it and found a half-gallon of unsweet tea along with deli chicken, cheese, and mayonnaise.

“Someone has done some digging into me, I see,” Kein said aloud. “And I’ll bet there’s a loaf of bread in here,” he added as he opened the pantry door.

There it was on the shelf—a brand-new loaf of bread.

He finished walking through the house. One room had a desk, complete with a lamp and chair. Another had a bed with frilly sheets, made up and ready for guests, but it definitely looked as though it had never been slept in. The master bedroom held a large, oversized bed with plenty of pillows and a built-in bathroom. The bedroom set matched perfectly and clearly looked like Charlene had a hand in choosing it.

Kein made a sandwich. It was nice not having to go to the store right away. He ate while watching the local news. That night, he got cleaned up and lay down in bed. It was quite possibly the most comfortable mattress he had ever felt. It wasn’t long before he drifted into deep sleep, not moving for the rest of the night.

The next morning, Kein woke feeling well rested. The room was still dark. He checked his phone—it was past eight o’clock. He opened the curtains and let the sunlight bleed into the room. He loved the sunlight; it was a wonderful reminder of God’s glory and grace. There was snow on the ground, and birds bounced around in the shrubs outside his window.

Kein showered, got dressed, and had another sandwich for breakfast. He put on his coat and stepped outside to explore the town, hoping to find the nearest grocery store and see what else was nearby.

Father Kein took off around the corner, passing all sorts of shops and stores. He passed quite a few people along the way; the town was bustling, and everyone seemed joyful.

“Christmas time,” he thought to himself.

Many greeted him with, “Good morning, Father,” which was a welcome change from his first days in Williamstown. He passed a pawn shop, a small coffee shop, and several clothing boutiques. At the end of the street, he found a grocery store.

“Not far–just a block over. That’s nice,” Kein said to himself.

He walked inside to look around. Fresh produce, well-stocked shelves, and a deli in the back. He smiled when he saw a stack of satsumas, grabbed a small bag and selected a few.

After paying, Kein walked next door to the local café. He stepped inside to have a cup of tea and take everything in. A waitress approached his table.

“Good morning, Father. What can I get you?”

“Yes, ma’am, good morning to you as well. My name’s Father Kein Laimend. How are you today? I think I’d like a cup of coffee—black, please.”

“I’m good–looking forward to getting off this afternoon. I get to pick up Mary, my youngest, from preschool for Christmas vacation. She gets the whole month off. Just the coffee, Father?”

“Yes, ma’am, thank you. The whole month? Wow, I’ll bet she’s excited,” Kein said with a smile. He loved seeing the joy of Christmas in children.

"Oh yeah, she definitely is. My name's Kathy—Kathy Stevens."

"Well, it's a pleasure to meet you, Kathy. You said your youngest—how many do you have?" Kein asked.

"Just two. My other one's a freshman in high school. Their dad and I didn't plan for the second, but you know what they say about telling God your plans," Kathy laughed.

"Yes, ma'am, I know exactly what you mean," Kein laughed.

When she returned with his drink, he noticed her wedding band.

"Well, it was a pleasure meeting you, Kathy. I presume I'll see you at Mass on Sunday?"

"Yes, of course, Father. We don't miss a single week unless someone's sick."

"I look forward to seeing you and your family," Kein said, placing a five-dollar bill on the table. "Keep the rest, Kathy."

She thanked him, and when he finished his coffee, Kein continued exploring town. He passed the grocery store and turned down the next street. There was a bookstore on the corner, a new-age shop halfway down, and a fresh food market on the next corner that looked like a farmer's market. He was pleased by how many people acknowledged him as Father. It truly seemed like a good town filled with good people.

As he returned home, he noticed the white Cadillac parked out front, though no one was inside. He walked up to find his door unlocked and Charlene inside, talking on the phone.

"Oh my goodness, there you are, Father. Let me go—he just walked in," she said before hanging up. "I knocked, but you didn't answer, so I let myself in to check on you—and you weren't here!" she said frantically.

"Mrs. Charlene, I'm not quite sure how to address this. Why are you in my house? I just went to the store to grab some oranges," Kein said.

"Well, no one told me you liked oranges. I could have had those here for you if I'd known."

"Charlene," Kein began gently, "I appreciate your kindness, but I think I'd like to get my own groceries, if you don't mind."

"Oh, I see. Well then, may I drive you to the Cathedral today? I'm sure you have a lot to do."

"Yes, Charlene. That would be very helpful."

"Okay then, Father. I'll just wait in the car," she said with a huff.

"Charlene, may I have your copy of the key to my house, please?" Father Kein asked. "I don't feel comfortable with someone I just met having full access to where I live. I understand the Church trusts you—it's just a personal space thing. You understand?"

Charlene removed the key from her ring. "Oh, no—I understand, Father. I didn't mean to come across too strongly. I'm just really excited you're here. I heard what you did in Williamstown, and I feel fortunate you're here to lead us closer to God."

She handed him the key and walked out to her car.

"How does she know all this about me?" Kein wondered aloud.

They drove to the Cathedral and inside, Kein made his way up to the choir loft. Taking it all in, he sat at the piano and began to play. It had been a long time, but his fingers fell naturally into place. The music filled the nave, echoing perfectly. His mind settled; for a moment, there was nothing but music and God.

When he finished, he looked down at Charlene.

“Mrs. Baker, would you be able to help me up here?”

She hurried up the stairs. “Yes, Father. What can I do?”

“If you wouldn’t mind, could you grab the cleaning supplies and give the piano a good cleaning? Dust on the wires can dull the sound of beauty.”

“Oh, I can call my cleaning lady—”

“No,” Kein interrupted gently. “I’d really appreciate it if you’d do it. I don’t know many people yet, and I can see you have a good heart. Just a deep cleaning—no polish.”

“Well, yes, Father. I can do that,” she said, as she started walking off.

Kein smiled and returned to the front of the church, bowing to the crucifix. He knelt behind the altar and prayed—for peace, for the homeless, for Williamstown, his friends, and Sandy. He prayed for over an hour. When he stood, he took a deep breath. It felt right to be here, like this was where he belonged.

His head began to ache again. He took two Tylenol and made a mental note to find a pharmacy soon. Redmond wasn’t large; it shouldn’t be difficult.

“I’m going to go for a walk to clear my head and prepare for Mass,” he told Charlene.

"Oh, I can drive you if you need."

"No, thank you. I'll just go around the block."

As he left, Kein realized Charlene needed tasks—something to stay busy. He walked the opposite direction from his house, enjoying the cool air. It was Wednesday, and he wanted his first homily to be meaningful. This week was the Second Sunday of Advent—the Feast of Saint Nicholas—and the anticipation of Christmas filled him with excitement.

The reading was from Matthew 9:35–10:1. It spoke of Jesus' compassion for the harassed and helpless and His sending of the disciples to heal and cast out demons. Kein wanted to bring Christ to this town, to help people grow in faith. That was all he ever wanted—to help people become better versions of themselves.

When he snapped out of his thoughts, he realized he'd walked farther than expected. A quiet neighborhood lay ahead, filled with the sounds of life—cars, voices, children playing.

"School must have let out," he murmured, checking his watch. "Half past three. Time to head back."

The fresh air cleared his mind, and by the time he returned to the Cathedral, he was able to write his homily. Charlene was waiting, the piano spotless. Kein nodded approvingly and she beamed.

She drove him home and asked, "Same time tomorrow?"

"I think I'll walk. It's only a mile, and the air here is wonderful."

"Oh... okay," she said, clearly disappointed.

That night, Father Laimend slept well. In the morning, his white Mustang arrived. He signed the papers, parked it in the garage, and smiled.

It wasn't until the delivery truck pulled out that he noticed a strange symbol on the sidewalk. Circles and an arrow, drawn in black. He brushed it away with his foot.

Charcoal, he thought to himself.

He dismissed it as not important and then he headed to the Cathedral, where the white Cadillac already waited.

Chapter 3

Signs and Symbols

It was now Saturday, and Kein was excited. This weekend would be his first Mass to celebrate, and he was prepared. He had spent time cleaning and organizing his things in the Cathedral. His parish seemed happy with him; everyone in town was kind and excited to have him there. He had met so many wonderful people. Everything was going wonderfully.

The Saturday evening Mass was filled with the afternoon crowd, composed mostly of the older generation and those who likely worked on Sundays. There were two readers, a married couple named Bill and Danielle, who read the first and second readings. Then Father Kein read from Matthew.

The next morning, the Cathedral was packed. There was some room in the back pews, but not much. It looked as though the whole town had shown up to worship. Father Laimend knelt in the Sacristy and prayed. He thanked God for providing him with such a wonderful opportunity to teach and lead. He thanked God for the beautiful Cathedral and for working through him to reach people. Most of all, he thanked God for his health and well-being, for the good weather, for all the help he had received, and for being able to help others.

He walked to the front of the church and began his approach to the altar, following his two altar servers. They were well taught; they knew all the signals and when to stop. After the two readings by Bill and Danielle again, he stepped up to the microphone and read from Matthew once more.

Kein closed the book and stood for a moment, staring in awe at his parish—his flock—whom he had been chosen to lead to Jesus. Then he began the homily.

He spoke about how often people feel lost, how often they long for relief from the weight of the world. He admitted that even he had felt lost at times. He explained how Jesus saw the crowds as helpless, harassed not only by illness and spiritual affliction but by oppression and cruelty, even from their own people. Kein spoke about Jesus telling His disciples that there were many ready to receive help, yet far too few willing to offer it. He explained that Christ sent His followers out to heal, to cast out evil, and to bring others to God.

Kein challenged the congregation to consider how often they had seen those less fortunate and turned away, rather than inviting them in—offering help, food, or faith. He reminded them that this was the calling of the Christmas season: not the exchange of worldly gifts, but the sharing of something eternal. The gift Jesus offered was everlasting life, not of this world, but of heaven. That, Kein said, was the gift that truly kept on giving—and the one he encouraged them to share with anyone willing to receive it.

After sharing the Eucharist, Kein stood at the back of the church and shook hands with the congregation. People spoke warmly to him.

"That was a wonderful message, Father."
"Great service, Father."
"It's just wonderful to have you here."

Then he saw Kathy with her two children in tow, the youngest being the preschooler. Kein smiled.

"It's so nice to see you here this morning, and this must be the one who has the whole month off for Christmas?"

Mary smiled shyly and turned her head away.

"She's shy, Father—don't pay her no mind," Kathy said. "And this is my oldest, Eli. He's the freshman."

Kein looked up at the teenager as he shook Eli's hand. "Well, what a lovely family. How are you doing, young man?"

“I’m doing good, Father. I really enjoyed your service today. I served here as an altar boy when I was younger.”

“That’s wonderful. Tell me, do you play ball for the Robins at the high school?”

“No sir. I didn’t try out this year. I’m thinking about it next year, though. I prefer basketball over football. I was never big enough to keep up with those guys.”

“He’s been spending a lot of time with friends and focusing on his schoolwork this year, Father,” Kathy added.

“I see. Well, you’re tall enough for it. Good luck with that, young man,” Kein said.

They left through the front doors, and Kein watched the people file out—some in cars, some on foot. Kathy and her children walked away together.

I wonder where her husband was today, Kein thought. *Maybe working.*

What a wonderful morning, he reflected—people seeking a closer relationship with Jesus, praying for one another, and welcoming him so openly.

Turning back inside, Kein saw Charlene and Ronald straightening the hymnals in the pews. He reached out and shook Ronald’s hand.

“Thank you both so much for staying and helping—and for all the assistance getting around town this week.”

“Of course,” Ronald said. “And please, call me Ron. Charlene has been raving about you.”

“She’s been a wonderful help,” Kein replied, “and has certainly clued me in on all the goings-on in town.”

“Yeah,” Ron laughed. “She’s good at that.”

“I can finish up here,” Kein said. “Why don’t you both go enjoy a nice lunch?”

“Oh, Father, we always help straighten things,” Charlene said.

Ron cut in, “I agree with Father Laimend. Let’s go get something to eat. I need to take my medicine on a full stomach anyway.” He winked at Kein.

“I’ll see you tomorrow, Father,” Charlene said as Ron nearly dragged her through the doors.

Kein finished tidying up—returning books to their places and straightening the bulletins. A deep sense of joy settled over him, and he sat in a pew to pray. He truly loved prayer; it was a pure and intimate way to speak with God.

When he finally stood to lock up, his vision suddenly went dark. He stumbled to his knees as his head began to pound so violently he couldn’t hear his own thoughts. He fumbled in his pocket for his Tylenol, spilling the entire bottle across the marble floor. He lay down, the cold stone soothing against his skin. Reaching out, he found a few pills, swallowed them, and closed his eyes, pleading silently for relief.

Then he heard a voice.

“Luke fifteen.”

Kein sat up slowly as the pain began to subside. He walked unsteadily to the altar and picked up his Bible. He knew Luke well—but which part of the chapter?

"Lord," he whispered, "please help me understand. Where do you need me to be?"

Suddenly the pain returned, sharper than before, shooting down his neck as he collapsed to his knees again.

"Three."

The word echoed through the pain.

"That's the story of the shepherd leaving the ninety-nine for the one," Kein murmured through tears.

He lay there with his eyes closed, waiting for the medicine to take effect before he dared to move again.

About an hour went by before Kein could stand fully. He remained at the altar, thinking about the verse, reading it silently to himself. In it, Jesus spoke of the shepherd who would leave the ninety-nine to search for the one that had gone astray and of the joy found in recovering what was lost. Kein exhaled slowly.

"What are you trying to tell me?" he whispered. "Am I meant to look for the lost sheep here in Redmond?"

It didn't make sense. Nearly everyone in Redmond attended Church. People lived the Word, or at least tried to. It was a Godly town—peaceful, faithful, welcoming. He closed the front doors of the Cathedral, tightened his coat, and began the walk home.

Halfway there, he changed his mind and took a detour toward the café near the grocery store. He hadn't eaten there before, only enjoyed a cup of coffee, and something about the place had stuck with him. As he approached, he read the sign aloud.

"Hideaway Café."

Inside, the air was warm and crowded, still buzzing from the lunch rush. Checkered tablecloths covered the tables, and the thick smell of barbecue filled the room. Kein took a seat near the window. A young woman approached, smiling.

“Good afternoon, Father. That was a great message today,” she said warmly. “I really liked how you talked about Jesus sending the disciples to people they didn’t even like—Gentiles and all—and telling them to heal and help anyway. It really shows how we’re supposed to love each other, no matter where we come from.”

Kein smiled. “Thank you. I’m glad it spoke to you.”

“What can I get you to drink?”

“An unsweet tea, please.”

She nodded. “Coming right up. I’m Cindy, if you need anything.”

She returned quickly with the tea, and Kein took a long sip, letting it settle before speaking again.

“What would you recommend here?”

“If it’s your first time, you have to try the barbecue pork steak,” Cindy said. “It’s what the state’s known for, and Hideaway does it best—if you ask me.”

“Well then,” Kein said, smiling, “I’ll trust you.”

As she turned to leave, he added, “And your interpretation of today’s reading was wonderful. Scripture speaks differently to each person, and you captured that beautifully.”

Cindy blushed. “Thank you, Father. That really means a lot.”

While he waited, Kein slipped two pills from his pocket and washed them down with tea. The headache lingered, dull but persistent. He hoped food would help.

When the plate arrived, it was massive—an enormous pork steak steaming under the lights.

“This looks incredible,” Kein said. “Thank you.”

He cut into the meat, which nearly fell apart beneath the knife. Steam rose, rich and savory. The first bite melted in his mouth. He leaned back slightly, eyes closed, chewing slowly.

Halfway through the meal, he noticed Eli enter with two other boys. They slid into a corner booth, laughing and glued to their phones, engaged in the serious business of teenage conversation.

Kein finished his meal and asked Cindy for the check and a box.

“Oh no, Father,” she said quickly. “This one’s on me. You can’t come here for your first barbecue and pay for it. But I’ll bring you a box—plenty left for supper.”

He protested, but she wouldn’t hear it. After she walked away, Kein tucked a generous tip beneath his plate.

Before leaving, he stopped by the boys’ table.

“Good afternoon, Eli. How are you?”

Eli looked up, grinning. “Good afternoon, Father. These are my friends Doug and Dillon. They moved here over the summer.”

Doug, red-haired and freckled, nodded. “I really liked your reading today.”

"Well, it was nice meeting you both," Kein said. "Eli, your friends seem like good company."

"They are," Eli said. "Mom's busy this afternoon, so we're hanging out."

Kein smiled. "Enjoy yourselves."

He thanked Cindy once more on his way out and quietly asked her to bring the boys dessert—on him—without saying where it came from. She promised she would.

Outside, the air had grown colder. He walked past the grocery store where he saw a familiar face through the window. He waved to Kathy with a smile and continued home.

That evening, he ate the rest of the pork steak, took more medicine, and collapsed into bed. Exhaustion overtook him—not just physical, but something deeper, heavier.

Sleep came fast.

Kein found himself standing on a dirt road, sheer rock cliffs rising on both sides. Sheep surrounded him—dozens of them—bleating softly. Ahead, a shepherd stood with his staff, counting.

Kein called out, but the shepherd did not respond.

The shepherd frowned, counted again, then turned and walked toward a narrow opening between the rocks.

Kein followed.

Inside, it was dark. He stumbled, striking his head on stone, tripping over uneven ground. At last, light appeared ahead. He emerged onto a narrow ledge.

The shepherd stood there, silent, wind pulling at his head wrap, staff planted firmly in the earth.

Below them was nothing but darkness.

“Where am I?” Kein asked. “Who are you?”

No answer.

The shepherd slowly raised his arm and pointed.

At the end of the path, a lamb was tangled in briars.

“Do you want me to help?” Kein asked as he edged towards the lamb. “Is that why I’m here?”

The wind howled louder. Dust filled the air. The lamb seemed farther away with every step. The ground shifted beneath Kein’s feet.

He slipped.

“FATHER!” he cried as he fell into the abyss.

Kein jolted upright in bed, drenched in sweat. His stomach churned. His heart pounded.

This was a message—he knew that much—but its meaning escaped him.

The clock read 3:00 a.m.

He lay back down, staring at the ceiling, whispering the Lord's Prayer over and over, asking for guidance until dawn began to break.

Chapter 4

Something's Wrong

It was Christmas Eve, and Laimend was preparing for midnight Mass. The tires of the white Cadillac sloshed through fresh snow, reminding him why he had agreed to let Charlene chauffeur him through the rest of winter—especially at night. He loved Christmas. Decorations were everywhere, reminders of the season: lights, shiny trees glowing in windows, and angels mounted on the streetlamps.

It had been several weeks since Laimend had taken over the Cathedral, and he had developed a good feel for everyone in town. He was settling in nicely and expected a strong turnout for Mass that night.

Charlene interrupted his thoughts from across the car. "So, I have the cookies and milk set up in the hall and of course the drop box for any last-minute letters to Santa. The kids really love getting response letters after Christmas."

"Yeah, I just don't understand why we're putting it up the night before Christmas," Kein said.

"Well, the kids sometimes forget what they wanted to ask for and this gives them a chance to still send it. I'll take care of the response letters, Father. They always get the same paragraph—something like, 'I didn't get this letter in time,' or 'I was already in the sky when you sent it.' Then Santa explains he'll put it on the list for next year. Of course, the parents then have an opportunity to make that happen," Charlene explained.

"I see. Well, it's definitely a unique tradition, but I understand the need for it," Kein said.

They walked into the nave, and Kein found his altar servers, assigning them their tasks as the music began. Father Kein proudly started his procession toward the sanctuary, singing along with the choir. The microphone around his ears projected his voice through the speakers, allowing it to echo beautifully throughout the Cathedral. He nodded to Eli and his mother as he passed. The room was filled with smiles and quiet joy.

During the Eucharist, Father Kein stood at the front of the congregation, distributing the Body of Christ. He smiled at Cindy as he placed it in her hands, placed one on Kathy's tongue, and then blessed Mary. He handed one to Eli and smiled as the boy consumed it and made the sign of the cross. Charlene and Ron were near the end of the line, patiently making their way toward him.

After giving them Communion, he noticed a familiar face behind them—a young woman with red hair approaching with a smile. His own smile widened as he realized it was Darby. He gave her the Body of Christ, and she returned to her seat.

After Mass, Father Kein wished everyone a Merry Christmas. Charlene waited near the front of the Cathedral as Laimend sat beside Darby and wrapped her in a warm hug.

"Darby, what are you doing here?"

"Well, since things in Williamstown have calmed down, I decided to take a small vacation and visit my cousin. She lives a town over, but I knew you were here, and I couldn't miss the chance to hear your homily," Darby said with a smile. "Besides, it's Christmas Eve—I can't sleep on Christmas Eve. I might miss Santa."

Kein laughed. "It really is so good to see you. What a wonderful surprise. How are things in Texas?"

"Ahem."

A ruffled voice came from the front doors. "Father, are you ready to head home yet?" Charlene asked.

"Um, no, Charlene. I think I'm going to stay here for a bit and catch up, if you don't mind," Kein replied.

"Well, Ron already left, so I guess I'll just wait here for you."

"No need to trouble yourself, Mrs. Baker," Kein said. "I think Darby can give me a ride—if you don't mind. It's only a mile or so down the road."

"Oh, no problem at all. I can do that," Darby said.

"Charlene, this is Darby—from Williamstown, Texas. She was part of my last parish," Laimend said as Darby stood to shake hands.

"Well, it's nice to meet you," Charlene said. "I'll see you tomorrow, Father." She walked out the doors, her red scarf flipping over her shoulder, without giving Darby a chance to respond.

"Tough crowd, huh, Father?" Darby said.

"She means well," Kein replied. "She just wants everyone to know she's doing a good job."

"I don't know," Darby said with a grin. "Seems like she's got a jealous bone in her."

"Oh no—she's married to Ronald," Kein laughed.

"I meant your time and attention, not a love interest, Father," Darby said, laughing.

They talked until nearly three in the morning—about Williamstown, how much Father Laimend was missed there, and how his new position was going. Darby spoke about enjoying the colder weather and how quaint the town felt. They exchanged phone numbers, like old friends reconnecting, and Laimend cherished the time with someone whose life he had once helped shape.

After locking up the Cathedral, Darby drove Kein home. When the car stopped, they both fell silent.

Painted across the garage door was a massive black symbol—a large circle filled with pentagrams, strange lines, and unfamiliar markings surrounding it.

"What... what is that, Father?" Darby's voice trembled.

"I—I don't know," Kein said, equally shaken. "Darby, would you mind calling the local police department?"

"Of course."

As Darby made the call, Kein stepped out of the car and began taking photos. The symbol was taller than he was—enormous. He took wide shots and close-ups, documenting every detail. When he touched one of the lines, it smeared easily, chalky beneath his finger. He sniffed it. It smelled like charcoal—maybe fireplace ash.

"The police are on the way," Darby said, startling him.

"Good. Thank you," Kein replied, still dazed.

"Merry Christmas—really early," Officer Dunberry said as he stepped out of his patrol car. "Can you tell me what happened?"

Kein explained the sidewalk incident and what he had discovered upon returning home.

"So why didn't you report the first one?" the officer asked.

“Honestly, I hadn’t been here long. I thought it was kids with chalk or something I hadn’t noticed before. But this—this wasn’t here before Mass,” Kein said. “Darby can confirm my whereabouts.”

“I believe you, Father,” the officer said. “I was at Mass tonight.”

“I thought I saw a uniform in the back,” Kein said with a faint smile.

After photos and statements, the officer said, “It looks like some kind of prank—maybe occult stuff, like you see in movies. I’m no expert, but we’ll look into it.”

Darby eventually left, and Kein sat on his porch until dawn, replaying his dream and the symbol in his mind.

As morning came, he wanted to make sure the town didn’t see this drawing on his garage. He stood on a chair and cleaned the graffiti easily. But as he lifted the chair to put it away, a blinding pain shot through his head and down his spine. He collapsed to his knees.

Then a hand caught him.

Voices blurred together.

And through the chaos, he heard God’s voice—indistinct, powerful.

Warmth surrounded him.

Darkness followed.

“Father. Father Laimend, can you hear me?” The voice was female. “Father, can you open your eyes for me?”

Kein opened his eyes slightly and saw a female paramedic kneeling beside him. He had been out for a while. He was on his couch. Looking around, he noticed a second paramedic at his feet, holding them steady. Charlene knelt in the corner of the living room, deep in prayer. Ron stood near the gurney, ready to help however he could.

“Yes, I can hear you,” Kein said.

“Good. Can you tell me where you are?”

“In my house.”

“What day is it?” the paramedic continued.

“Christmas,” Kein replied.

“Good. Okay, I want you to lie here for a bit. Let me get some vitals,” she said, shining a light into his eyes. The brightness worsened the pain in his head, but he didn’t say anything. She checked his blood pressure and temperature. “Everything looks like it’s returning to normal. Father Laimend, we need to take you to the hospital to get you checked out. Can you try to stand up for me?”

“I’m not going to the hospital,” Kein said calmly. “I just got dizzy after being on the chair cleaning. I’m okay—just give me a minute.”

“No, I don’t think so, Father. I really want to take you in and have you checked.”

“I understand,” Kein said, “but my vitals are fine, and I’m not driving anywhere. I don’t believe you can force me to go. I do appreciate your concern—truly—but please give me a moment.”

He could hear the second paramedic explaining to Charlene that they couldn't force him to go since he was lucid and his vitals were normal.

"Father, you really need to go," Charlene said, her voice cutting through the room.

"I appreciate your concern," Kein said as he sat up. "But I don't think I need to go. I feel better now."

The paramedics continued to argue and persuade for a while, but Kein's mind was made up. He wasn't going to the emergency room. After promising to call if anything changed—and agreeing to let Charlene check on him later that afternoon—the paramedics finally left.

"Thank you both again for being in the right place at the right time," Laimend said to Ron and Charlene.

"What were you doing on that chair anyway?" Charlene asked, clearly frustrated. "You could have fallen and broken something."

"Well, I was cleaning my garage door. It had some—"

"Cleaning your garage door?" Charlene interrupted. "What in the world for? I could have had people come clean whatever you wanted!"

"I understand that," Laimend said gently, "but I am quite capable of doing things myself, Charlene." He paused. "Besides, what are you both doing here? It's Christmas Day. Aren't you supposed to be with your family?"

"Well, we were on our way out of town to see the grandkids," Charlene said, reaching for a small package wrapped in silver and gold paper. "But we wanted to drop this off first."

A tag on the gift read:

To: Father Kein Laimend
From: Ron and Charlene Baker

Thank you so much for coming to our town.

He opened the gift slowly, cautiously excited—Christmas was his favorite time of year. Inside, beneath bubble wrap, was a stainless-steel cup engraved with:

World's Best Priest's Tea.

Don't Touch!

"This is one of the nicest things anyone has ever given me," Kein said, standing to hug them both. "Thank you so much. I truly appreciate it."

"Well, you drink so much tea," Charlene said, "I thought something to keep it cold would be helpful."

"Come on, Charlene," Ron said, holding the door open. "Let's get to the kids and let Father Laimend rest. Merry Christmas, Father."

"Father," Charlene added as they stepped out, "you promise you'll call if you need anything—anything at all?"

"Yes, ma'am," Kein said. "I promise. I'll see you this afternoon when you come by to check on me. Enjoy your day."

When they left, Kein sat back down on the couch, smiling at the cup in his hands. It was genuinely thoughtful of them to think of him on Christmas. He poured himself a glass of unsweet tea, sealed the lid, and flipped through the channels until he found the Christmas Day parade—his favorite.

He tried to forget everything that had happened over the past few hours, but his mind wouldn't let him enjoy the program. It kept returning to the symbol on his garage door.

Thank goodness Charlene didn't see that, he thought. *She would've called the National Guard.*

He chuckled softly, then frowned. *But she saw me on the chair—and she tends to drive by unannounced. She must have seen it. Unless... she didn't.*

His thoughts raced. Why wouldn't she ask about it—unless she truly hadn't seen it?

Then his mind returned to the dream. And to God's voice—heard through the chaos as he was helped inside. He hadn't understood it at the time, but now pieces were coming together.

"Help..." "Lamb..." "Call..."

Only fragments—but enough to trouble him. *Help the lamb? Call for help for the lamb?* Who was the lamb? Who needed him?

Kein didn't know exactly what was being asked of him, but one thing was clear: God was calling him to help someone here in Redmond.

He picked up his phone and opened the photos of the garage door. The lines were rough, uneven—applied by hand or stick. Zooming in, he could see the grainy texture. Ashes, he was certain. No residue on the ground. No footprints. And the height—he'd needed a chair to clean it.

The symbols inside the circle unsettled him. Aside from the pentagram, he didn't recognize them. They made him uneasy, but he reminded himself that he was here for a reason—and God would protect him.

He finished his tea, feeling clearer now, his head much improved. Carrying the cup to the sink, he suddenly stopped.

He knew exactly what to do.

Kein hurried back to his phone, attached the photos, and typed:

Hello, my old friend. How are you? Merry Christmas. I hate to send something like this on Christmas Day, but I need your help. Can you tell me what these drawings are—or at least point me in the right direction? Thank you, my friend. I hope you have a wonderful day.

He hit send and set the phone down.

It rang before he even made it back to the kitchen.

Kein smiled as he answered.

"Hello."

Chapter 5

Trouble Bags

"Hello, my old friend. How are you doing over there in the cold weather?" Rozas laughed through the phone. "Ha! Merry Christmas to you too. And what is this stuff you're sending me?"

"Wow, I really didn't realize how good it would be to hear your voice, Rozas," Kein said, overjoyed to hear his friend on the other end of the line. "I hope everything is going well in Texas for you. I was hoping you could lend me some help with that stuff. I seem to be at a loss as to what it is—and what it means."

"Well, of course, my friend. I'd be glad to take a look at it. Are you having some trouble?"

"No, no trouble—just confusion, really," Kein replied.

"I'll do some digging and see what I can come up with. Hopefully I can get you some answers this week. So, tell me—how is Mrs. Baker treating you?" Rozas asked, a hint of sarcasm in his voice.

"YOU KNOW HER?" Kein exclaimed.

"Ha! I made some contacts before you left. I just wanted to make sure you were well taken care of. She was who Father Pete recommended I get in touch with. And let's just say—she was very happy to look after you. I could tell just by talking to her that you'd be in *good* hands!" Rozas let out a hearty laugh.

"You told her to keep an eye on me? You're the reason she knows all about me?" Kein laughed. "I owe you big time for this one, my friend." It felt good to laugh about something so small. "She's very nice and definitely helpful. I'd just describe her as... extra."

"Ha, yes—she sounded like that on the phone. I was just looking out for you, my friend," Rozas said with a chuckle.

“Well, I do appreciate you reaching out and making sure I had someone here to rely on. Walking to the Cathedral in the snow isn’t something I’d enjoy daily, so having her as a personal driver is nice sometimes.”

They talked for nearly half an hour before ending the call. Kein felt confident Rozas would be able to help him sort things out. That man knew people from all walks of life. He was the best contact Father Laimend had.

That afternoon, Ron and Charlene stopped by to check on Kein. Charlene looked surprised when he asked her about her conversation with Rozas.

“Well—uh—Father Pete spoke to me about you coming here, and then he put Monseigneur Rozas in touch with me. He was just looking out for your best interests,” Charlene said, stumbling over her words. “And when the Monseigneur told me about your... uh... condition, I knew I was the right person to help. With my availability and our devotion to the Church and all.”

“It’s alright, Mrs. Baker,” Kein said gently, smiling. “Rozas is a good friend of mine. He wants what’s best for me and for the Church. I’m very grateful he contacted you—and for everything you and Ron have done for me here in Redmond.”

“Well, we were honored to be asked. And I haven’t told anyone about your... head issue—except Ron, of course. I don’t think it’s right to spread people’s personal business,” Charlene said.

Kein thought briefly of how freely she had shared the town’s gossip during their first meetings. “Yes, well, I appreciate that as well.”

They shared leftovers from Christmas dinner that Charlene had brought back from her daughter's house. It was nice to have a home-cooked meal. Kein found himself more at ease around them now, his guard lowered after speaking with Rozas.

Charlene excused herself to the restroom before they left for the evening. Father Laimend felt content. His congregation was strong, his stomach was full, and his friend was helping him search for answers. He hadn't mentioned the dreams to Rozas—it didn't seem important at the time. Still, this Christmas was one he would remember for years.

That night, as Father Laimend lay in bed, his thoughts wandered. He wondered how long it would take Rozas to uncover something. He pictured the symbol on the garage door. He thought about the long, comforting conversation with Darby. Exhaustion finally overtook him after being awake for nearly twenty-four hours, and he drifted off before he realized it.

The shepherd appeared again, staring into Laimend's very being. The wind was unbearable. Kein raised his hands to shield his eyes from the blowing dust. The shepherd lifted his arm and pointed down the same path as before.

"What is it? What do I need to do?" Kein shouted.

At the cliff's edge, the same lamb struggled in the thorn bush. As Kein stepped forward, thorns grew before his eyes—longer, sharper—piercing the lamb's skin. Blood appeared, bright red against white wool. The lamb cried out in pain, thrashing helplessly.

Kein took another step, fighting the wind as it grew stronger. "I'M TRYING!" he shouted, turning back toward the shepherd—but he was gone.

When Kein turned again, the shepherd stood beside the lamb. Thorns wrapped tightly around its legs and feet. Kein stepped forward, but a violent gust shoved him backward. His feet slid toward the passageway entrance.

He pushed forward again, crying out, "GOD, HELP ME! GIVE ME THE STRENGTH TO HELP THEM!"

The wind answered by throwing him back.

Then a voice rose from the thorn bush—deep, booming, dark.

"This one is mine. You cannot save it."

Kein was blown over the edge.

"FATHER! SAVE ME! PLEASE—HELP ME!"

Father Laimend woke to daylight. Tears streamed down his face. He could still feel the wind on his skin, the dust burning in his eyes. It had been too vivid—too real.

He sat up and placed his feet on the floor.

Dust covered the ground beside his bed.

"It was real," he whispered.

He knelt and touched it with his fingers. Immediately, he began to pray for guidance—desperate for direction, for understanding.

"God, hallowed be Thy name. You are the King of the universe, Lord over all. I ask for Your guidance. Help me understand what You are showing me. Show me the path I must take. I am Yours to shape and mold according to Your will. Use me as You see fit. Carry me to where I am most useful to You. Your will be done. In Your name, Father Almighty. Amen."

Kein stood and stared at the dust near his feet.

A breeze stirred beneath the bed.

The dust lifted and vanished before his eyes, as if it had never existed.

Was he imagining it?

Kein's chest tightened.

Was his condition worsening? Was the tumor growing faster than the doctors had expected?

He quickly made his way to the bathroom to wash his face, hoping it would help him wake up. The cold water splashing against his skin was refreshing, and he could feel himself coming back to reality. Still, all he could think about was the dream and what it could mean.

What was the lamb's blood? It hadn't been there in the first vision. It had to be a vision—this was far more than a dream. The thorns were too real, stained red with blood. The shepherd had been in a different place this time. Kein had seen his face more clearly. He had a beard, and he was old—but not old in years. He looked as though he belonged to another time entirely.

Laimend finished drying his face with the towel and opened the medicine cabinet to grab some Tylenol. His head was pounding so badly he could feel it in his stomach. As Kein reached for the bottle, he noticed something small and brown tucked into the corner.

"Hmmm, I don't recall seeing that before," Kein said to himself as he pulled it out and set it on the sink.

It was a small burlap bag, tied at the top with twine. On the outside was one of the symbols again.

Kein stepped back in horror. "What is this?" he asked aloud, his face frozen in confusion.

Slowly, he untied the bag and opened it. A horrible stench rose from inside. He turned it over into the sink, and immediately Father Kein dropped the bag onto the floor. He stared at the contents: small bones, a red substance, and a rock of some kind in the midst of various other things.

This was too much.

He grabbed his phone and took several pictures, then immediately sent a folder of them to Rozas, hoping he hadn't woken him. After that, Kein did the only thing he could think to do. He dialed Darby's number.

"Hello, Father. How are you doing after Christmas Day? Is everything okay?" Darby asked.

"No, Darby, I don't think so. Something is happening here, and I don't know what to do. I just found a bag of something in my bathroom."

"A bag? Like clothes or something? Father, are you experiencing some memory loss?"

"No, Darby. Like bones. A small bag of bones and other things."

"Oh my God. Father, did you call the cops back? They need to see this too. I'm turning around—I'll head your way," Darby said, her voice tightening.

"No, Darby. I just need to talk to someone I trust. Let me calm down a bit and I'll be fine."

"No, that's not going to work for me, Father. I'm calling Dan at the café and letting him know I'll be out a few more days." Darby hung up.

Kein's phone rang immediately.

"Hello?"

"My friend, what is that?" Rozas asked, worry heavy in his voice. "That doesn't look normal. Where was it?"

"In my bathroom. Inside my house, Rozas. I need to know what this is as soon as possible. Please tell me you've found something on the other drawing—anything!" Kein was panicking now.

"I'm expecting some information today or tomorrow. Relax. I'll call Charlene and have her come sit with you."

"No. Don't," Kein said quickly. "I don't think I trust her. What do you really know about her, Rozas?"

"Not much. Father Pete recommended her, and that was enough for me. I trust him completely. Why, Kein?"

"Because she was in my bathroom last night after I had that attack yesterday. She didn't see what was on the garage door, but somehow, she and Ronald were here at exactly the right time when I fell. I don't get a good feeling about her."

There was a pause. “Then I’ll make preparations to come to you, Father. We’ll figure this out together.”

“No. Darby is already on her way, and she’s much closer. Just please—find out what this is and what it means.”

“I will, my friend. Don’t go outside today,” Rozas said before hanging up.

About two hours later, Darby arrived at Kein’s house. He was grateful she had been close enough to return so quickly. This didn’t feel like a random incident—it felt targeted. He had dealt with demons before, directly and indirectly, but never like this. Never aimed at him.

The door creaked as he opened it for Darby. They embraced, and then Kein pulled out his phone and showed her the pictures.

“Father… what is that?” Darby asked.

“I don’t know. But I’m sure it was meant for me to find. I think God is pointing me somewhere—I just can’t see it yet.”

“It looks like bad juju to me.”

“Ju-ju?” Kein asked, confused.

“There’s stuff like this across the border from Texas. Not even that far into Mexico. Witchcraft—real bad stuff. Los Muertos.”

“The dead,” Kein said.

“Yes. Depending on how it’s used, it can help… or bring death right to your door. It’s not something anyone should mess with.”

“I agree. The Church is very clear about that. Even Scripture forbids necromancy and magic. How do you know all this?”

Darby hesitated, then spoke quietly. “I had a friend growing up. Her grandmother raised her in the craft. Rituals. Sacrifices. Blood covenants. She told me her grandmother could shapeshift.”

“She could what?” Kein said, stunned.

“Into animals. Owls. Deer. It’s common in that world.”

“Did you actually see it?”

“No. But I’ve seen enough to know the magic is real. And it terrifies me.”

“Darby,” Kein started to talk but she stopped him.

“I saw her grandmother cooking something in a pot one time. It was a thick, unnatural looking red mixture. Later, my friend told me it had the blood of a dead man in it, mixed with other things.

She took a leaf of lettuce and wrote a man’s name on it. Supposedly, he was the man who had gotten a girl pregnant—the girl had gone to her grandmother for help, or revenge, or something like that. She dipped the lettuce into the mixture, soaking it, then fed it to a goat.

The next day, the goat was violently sick—literally dying. It lasted about a day before it finally gave out. She threw the body into a fire.

A week later, the man went through the same cycle. He got terribly ill. A few days after that, he was dead. The doctors couldn’t figure out what caused it.

But the strangest part was what happened afterward. His wife had him cremated. His parents were furious—they cursed her for it. They said he never would have wanted that. They said he wanted to be buried.”

“That’s evil,” he said firmly. “Purely demonic.”

They returned to the bathroom and examined the contents.

“That’s chicken bones,” Darby said. “Eggshell or seashell fragments. That stone looks like tiger’s eye. And that’s dried blood.”

“Did you call the police?” she asked.

“I forgot,” Kein admitted. “I will now.”

When Officer Dunberry arrived, he examined the bathroom carefully.

“Father, someone broke into your house,” he said, pointing to the window latch. “Easy entry.”

Outside, muddy prints marked the wall. “See here, they climbed in from this point.”

“Yes, I didn’t think about looking out here.”

“They’re getting bolder,” the officer said. “Or sneakier.”

After taking photos, Dunberry paused, eyeing the evidence bag. “If I didn’t know better, I’d say this looks like fried chicken leftovers.”

After he left, Kein turned to Darby, pale. “Charlene brought me baked chicken from her daughter’s Christmas dinner.”

“Oh my God,” Darby whispered. “You have to tell Dunberry!”

“Not yet,” Kein said quietly. “I’m not ready.”

The phone rang.

Rozas confirmed it immediately. “That’s a hex bag Kein, it’s Old English magic. Salem-era practices. Really old stuff.”

Then came the final blow.

“The diocese knew,” Rozas said. “That’s why they sent you.”

Kein sat back slowly.

“That figures,” he said.

After the call ended, he looked at Darby. “We need to be sure it’s Charlene. And if it is, we need to know what she’s involved in—and who else might be.”

Darby nodded. “I agree, Father.”

Chapter 6

A False Saint

The next morning, Father Kein and Darby sat together, eating a breakfast comprised of a chicken sandwich with tea and working out a plan moving forward.

"You eat this for breakfast all the time?" Darby asked.

"Yes, why? You don't like it?" Kein asked, completely serious.

"Oh—uh—no, it's great, Father. I just never thought about a sandwich for breakfast, that's all," Darby said, trying to backtrack without laughing. "So, do you think Charlene would have something in her car, or maybe you could get into her house to see what's going on?"

"Before all this, I would've said yes without hesitation. But if she's behind this, I don't know how open she'd be to me snooping around her home. I *can* dig around in her car, though," Kein said. "I think I have an idea," he dialed Charlene's number.

"Hello, yes, Father. Well of course I can come pick you up—but didn't I see Darby still in town yesterday afternoon? Oh, I'm so sorry to hear that. Would you like me to bring something for her stomach? All right then, no problem, Father. I'll get ready and be there soon."

Charlene hung up the phone, and Kein stood from the couch with a tight smile.

He looked at Darby with a smirk. "I hate telling a fib, and I'll have to confess later, but it'll help me get the information I need. Are you sure you're okay with your part in this?"

"Not really, Father—but if it's the only way, then yes. I don't have to be happy about it," Darby replied.

"I know, Darby. I know. We're just fortunate that Ronald isn't retired."

Darby went to the spare bedroom and lay down to wait. It wasn't long before the white Cadillac pulled up outside, and a familiar knock echoed through Kein's home.

"Good morning, Mrs. Baker. I truly appreciate this."

"Good morning, Father. Let me check on her and see how she's feeling. I'm pretty good at figuring out what to cook to help someone feel better," Charlene said as she brushed past him and went down the hall.

She knocked lightly and peeked into the room. "Good morning, Darby. How are you feeling? Is there anything I can do?"

"No ma'am, it's just my stomach. I think I ate something bad," Darby said.

"Well, I can make you some good beef and vegetable soup to bring for supper. That always helps Mr. Baker's stomach aches."

"Oh, no ma'am, it's okay. It'll pass later. I just need to rest today. Maybe this afternoon I can get up and take Father Kein off your hands or something."

"No, I'm making it—and that's the end of that conversation. I'll just make an extra stop with Father Laimend to get the ingredients. It doesn't take long at all. Now, you get some rest, and if you need anything, I'll write my number down in the kitchen, dear."

"Okay, Mrs. Baker. I really appreciate that," Darby said, rolling onto her side.

Charlene returned to the living room, explained her plan and wrote her number on a scrap of paper from her purse before setting it on the counter.

"All right, Father, let's go. We'll get the ingredients after lunch, then stop by my house to grab my pots."

"Yes ma'am, that sounds good. And again, I truly appreciate you dropping everything to come get me today."

"Of course, Father."

They drove first to the Cathedral so Kein could make his daily rounds—straightening, praying, tending to small but important tasks. Charlene helped sweep and organize the Daily Bread books. They changed the altar cloth and checked the choir loft. It was menial work, but it mattered to Laimend—and more importantly, it took time.

Meanwhile, Darby rubbed her leg where her jeans had ripped climbing the fence into the Bakers' backyard. She wasn't familiar with breaking and entering, but she was willing if it meant helping Father Kein.

She tried the sliding glass door. Locked. Of course.

She slid her pocketknife toward the latch, but the gap was too tight. The door wouldn't budge. Stepping back, she scanned the house. To the right of the patio door was a small window, about four feet off the ground.

Just like Father Kein's bathroom, she thought.

She worked the blade under the window seam easily. *Officer Dunberry was right—this is easy*. She wiggled the knife, listening for a click. Nothing.

Frustrated, she pulled the knife out and leaned against the window.

It slid open.

“What? It’s freaking unlocked,” she whispered.

It was the bathroom. She eased her legs inside first, feeling for the floor. It shifted beneath her foot. The surface slid—and she fell sideways, groaning.

As she sat up, she saw a pair of men’s underwear tangled around her shoe.

“Tighty whities. Classic,” she muttered, gagging slightly as she kicked them off.

Meanwhile, Charlene parked near the café. “Father, we can grab groceries after we eat, but first, if it’s all right with you, I’m going to run into the store real quick—my daughter’s birthday is coming up.”

“Of course. I’ll wait here,” Laimend said.

“No, go ahead and get us a table. I won’t be long.”

“No ma’am,” Kein insisted. “It would be rude to start without you.”

Charlene nodded and walked off. Kein watched her enter the New Age store.

That’s telling, he thought.

He opened the glove box—nothing unusual. Then the center console. It was crammed. Breath mints. Tissues. Old photos.

Halloween pictures.

Charlene stood in a pointed witch's hat before a cauldron, flanked by two other women dressed the same. Ronald crouched inside the cauldron.

Not proof—but interesting.

"Can I help you find something, Father?"

Charlene's voice made him jump.

"I—I uh—was just looking for some gum. Hungrier than I thought," Kein stammered.

"I told you to go ahead without me," she laughed. "Come on, let's eat."

At the café, Kathy greeted them warmly. "Father, unsweet tea?"

"Yes, please."

"And Mrs. Baker, the usual?"

"That'll be fine, Kathy."

"Today's special is fried chicken with mashed potatoes and gravy."

"Is that what you're having?" Kein asked.

"Me? Lord, no. Far too greasy. I don't do anything with chicken—too many steroids these days. I'm having the Cobb salad."

"I'll try the special," Kein said.

As Kathy walked away, Kein felt uneasy. Charlene's words echoed in his mind—*I don't do anything with chicken.*

Yet she had brought him chicken on Christmas. And the bones in his house.

The pieces were beginning to form a very troubling picture. He watched Charlene tuck a large bill under the napkin holder. "I always try to help Kathy out. It's been hard on her since her husband passed away."

Back in the Bakers' home, Darby was having zero luck. She had gone through every inch of the back of the house and was now making her way through the living room—couch cushions, magazines, anything she could think of. Nothing. The kitchen had to have something. It had to.

She opened the refrigerator and began looking. Milk, eggs, juice, leftovers. Nothing out of the ordinary. Cabinets next—pots, pans, plates, silverware. Everything was neat. Normal. Too normal.

There was no evidence here.

She has to be doing this magic work somewhere else, Darby thought.

Then she heard voices at the front door.

Father Kein's voice hit her like ice water. They were back—earlier than she expected.

Darby bolted for the bathroom as the front door opened and Kein and Charlene walked inside. She pressed herself against the bathroom door, listening.

"I'm going to run to the restroom really quick, Father," Charlene said. "Then we can get the pots and go cook at your place."

"Oh... my... God," Darby whispered.

Footsteps moved down the hallway.

Darby scrambled to the window, shoved it open, and slipped through just as the bathroom door creaked. She slid the window shut as quietly as she could. A second later, she heard the door close and Charlene humming to herself.

"Whew," Darby breathed.

She climbed the fence, ignoring the tear in her jeans, and ran for her car parked around the corner. She had to beat them back.

Back at Laimend's house, Darby entered from the hallway as pots clanged in the kitchen, her adrenaline finally wearing off.

"Mrs. Baker, you really don't have to cook anything," she said. "I'm feeling much better now."

"Nonsense, dear," Charlene replied as she turned around. "And what happened to you? Your pants are ripped."

"Oh—yeah. I didn't realize," Darby said, glancing down at the fresh tear. "Must've missed that earlier."

Charlene sniffed. "Not very ladylike to wear around Father Laimend, but you young people do all sorts of things differently."

Kein cut in gently. “Darby, if you don’t mind, would you go change? Maybe we can get you a new pair in town tomorrow.”

Darby nodded and retreated, grateful for the excuse.

When she returned, the house smelled incredible—warm, comforting, like a hug. Charlene hummed at the stove, stirring. Father Kein stood nearby, watching, asking questions, trying to learn.

She really did seem like a perfectly kind woman. Nothing like the witches from movies.

“Anything else I can do to help, Mrs. Baker?” Kein asked. “If not, I’ll start on the dishes.”

“No, Father, I’m good,” Charlene said. “Just letting it simmer. Secret ingredient is V8 juice—kicks the flavor up a notch.”

“Yes ma’am, I’ll write that down—”

Kein’s phone rang.

“Yes... oh. Of course. That’s very interesting. Thank you for letting me know. You have a good evening.”

He hung up and turned to Darby. “Excuse us a moment, Charlene.”

He led Darby into the hall. “That was Officer Dunberry.”

“And?” Darby asked. “Anything that points to Charlene?”

“No. Forensics reviewed the muddy footprint. Size ten or eleven. Not even close to Charlene’s shoe size.”

“She could have an accomplice,” Darby said.

“Possibly. But I didn’t find anything in her car. Did you find anything at her house?”

Darby sighed. “Other than ripping my favorite pants and slipping on Mr. Baker’s underwear? No. And yes—I’m absolutely taking you up on those new pants.”

Kein glanced back toward the kitchen. Charlene was ladling red soup into bowls.

Kein approached her. “Charlene, may I ask what you bought at the store earlier?”

“My daughter’s birthday gift,” she said easily. “A wind chime with the moon and stars.”

Relief and confusion hit him at the same time.

“I was just curious,” Kein said.

“Oh, I don’t like that store at all,” Charlene added. “Too much nonsense in there. But my daughter loves wind chimes, and they happened to have the one I wanted here in stock,” she continued, “High school kids spend too much time in there for my liking.”

“High school kids?” Darby asked.

“Yes. That Stevens boy—Eli—and I see other kids from the school going there all the time.”

Charlene looked at them both and could see the wheels turning in their heads. “Well, you two clearly are trying to figure something out. I, need to get home and get Ron some supper started, so I'll leave you to it. Darby, I'm glad you're feeling better, let me know if you need anything else, Father."

The door closed behind her.

"Oh my God," Kein whispered. "Kathy told me Eli loved the fried chicken. He took an extra serving last week."

Darby's eyes widened. "The high school kid?"

"Yes. Shoe size matches. His father died." Kein was already dialing. "This is it, Rozas. It's not Charlene."

After the call, Kein pulled the curtain aside.

A red symbol stared back at him from the window—wet, dripping down the glass.

Kein stumbled backward.

"Father?" Darby shouted.

His vision narrowed. Darkness pressed in. He thought he saw a figure running down the street.

Then the floor rushed up.

His head shattered the glass tabletop.

Darby grabbed his phone and hit redial.

Kein's eyes closed and he could feel his skin moving with every throb of the headache that overtook him. Then nothing, he wasn't there anymore.

Chapter 7

THAT'S ENOUGH!

Laimend was standing on the ledge of the cliff, staring at the lamb now covered in its own blood from the thorns. The wind had all but ceased, and he was able to move close enough to touch the animal. He tried to pry away the thorns, but every time he moved it even a little, they only dug deeper into the lamb, and more blood covered the ground. The lamb was now almost entirely red, a stark contrast to the glorious white it once was.

The shepherd only stood there, staring down at Kein and the lamb. Kein pleaded for help from the shepherd. He left the lamb and moved to the shepherd on his hands and knees, begging. He prayed for help, guidance, and mercy for the animal.

Kein looked up from the shepherd's feet to see the face of Jesus staring back at him. He scrambled back. He didn't know if it was out of fear or reverence, but the warmth of ten suns filled his heart, and he was suddenly at peace with everything he had ever experienced. He looked up at Jesus and tried to speak, but the words wouldn't come. Then, as if Jesus was directly in his head, he heard the voice of God speaking to him.

"One of the one hundred is lost, ensnared in something they cannot comprehend and cannot escape. It is consuming them. Save them. Command my servants to save them."

Then silence.

Kein looked up, and the shepherd was gone. Jesus was gone. Only the lamb in the thorns remained, still struggling, bleeding. Then something happened—everything became darker. The bush took on a mind of its own, and it began to speak to Laimend in the most horrid voice.

"This one is mine; you can't save it because it doesn't want to be saved. See how it struggles, but only until it is comfortable enough to allow the thorns to remain. Run away, priest. Run away now. You have no power here. HA HA ha ha ha…"

The laughter faded as Kein felt the rush of the wind again, and he braced himself for the inevitable fall from the cliff, back into his own mind.

His eyes began to open slowly. He could see Darby on the phone, walking back and forth in his kitchen. He was still at home. He could smell the soup, still warm. He hadn't been out that long. He raised his hand and tried to speak, but his tongue wouldn't move.

"Yes, Monseigneur, yes," he could hear Darby speaking, to Rozas he assumed. "No, I'm not sure… He's moving, let me go, Monseigneur."

She hung up the phone and knelt down by Laimend. "Father, Father, can you hear me?"

Kein nodded his head.

"Are you ok? Can you talk?"

"Yeah," the word was slow to come as Darby helped him sit up against the couch. "Darby, I'm ok. I just need a minute and some Tylenol. Would you please get me some, in the cabinet over there?"

"Yes, Father, I think I need to call an ambulance. Monseigneur told me—"

"No, Darby," Kein cut her off. "That won't be necessary. Just a glass of tea, please, with the Tylenol, and then we can sit down for a bit."

Darby rushed to the kitchen, filled a glass with tea from the refrigerator, and came back with the Tylenol. Kein took the two pills and drank his tea slowly, trying to recover his footing. He stood up with her help and made his way to the kitchen table, then sat down.

“Darby,” he started, “it’s Eli. He’s the lost lamb. He’s the one into witchcraft.”

“Are you sure, Father? And what do you mean, lost lamb?”

“I’ll explain later, but yes, I’m sure now,” Kein responded.

“What do we do now?” she asked, uncertainty in her voice.

“You go home. I will handle the rest from here, Darby.”

“Absolutely not. I am in this as much as you are now, Father,” Darby said sternly. “And you aren’t going anywhere right now. You need to eat something and rest if you’re not going to the hospital.”

Kein slowly walked to the table and took a bite of the soup in his bowl. It was still warm. Surprisingly, it was very tasty, and he felt the energy coming back to him one tiny bit at a time.

“Tomorrow morning, we will go to Kathy’s house and talk with her and Eli. Maybe we can get the information we need to move forward then,” Kein said.

“Yes, I can agree to that, Father,” Darby said.

They finished the meal, and she helped Kein to his bed and shut the door. Darby sat on the couch alone and began to shake. It wasn’t from fear, but from the unknown. She had no idea what was coming next or what to do to stop it. She was worried about Father Laimend, and he was the only person in town she knew and trusted. She wanted to tell him to wait, that Rozas was on his way, but she knew Father Laimend was very headstrong about things. Her ability to slow him down was limited.

She cleaned up the broken glass, then fixed herself another bowl of soup and sat down to eat. Her mind was racing in all different directions. Her eyes grew heavy, and she fell asleep at the table without finishing her meal.

The next morning, Kein got up and saw Darby asleep at the kitchen table, leaning on one hand. He smiled to himself and began to get ready. He took a shower and cleaned up for the day. He knew it was going to be a long one. After he finished, he woke Darby up with a cup of coffee. Charlene had stocked some in his cabinet when he first moved there, but he hadn't opened it until now.

"Oh, good morning, Father. Did I sleep here all night? Geez, I'm sorry. I was just worried about things and—"

"It's ok, Darby. It's all perfectly fine. I can't express how much I appreciate your help yesterday and last night and for cleaning up my mess on the floor. I don't think I could have made it to bed without you, so thank you for that. Now today, after you get some coffee and breakfast, it's time for you to go home."

"Father, I'm not going home and that's final! I'm staying with you until help arrives, or you decide to take me with you. Only two ways this is happening, so you decide which," Darby said.

"I don't think you understand quite what is going to happen, Darby. I'm only going to have a conversation with the family, nothing more. The path forward will be decided once we have proof of whatever is going on, but this is the first step," Laimend responded, trying to sound calm.

"Then let's go have a conversation, Father." Darby stood up and then caught a whiff of herself. "Uh, after I shower and change clothes."

She made her way down the hallway to get ready for the day. Kein began to clean up the kitchen as he waited for her. He was sure she would follow him if he took off without her, and it was better if she drove him anyway. His mind was lost in the conversation to come. What would Kathy say? Would Eli confess to it? How far into this mess was he, and what about his friends?

"Too many questions right now. Just make the first step," he told himself.

Darby came walking down the hallway in a pair of black leather pants and a black leather jacket. Father Kein looked at her strangely, then turned toward the door.

"What? It's all I have left that ain't dirty, and besides, this is fashionable and warm," Darby said.

Laimend didn't respond. He just shook his head with a smile and walked out the door.

They arrived at Kathy's home just before 10 a.m., and Father Kein sat still for a second. He was praying to God for protection and guidance for both he and Darby. Then he turned to her and said, "Is there anything I can do to get you to stay in the car?"

"Nope. I'm glued to you, Father," she replied with a smile.

Father Kein sighed and got out of the car.

Kathy opened the door with her daughter, Mary, on her hip. "Good morning, Father. What brings you here today?"

"Kathy, would you mind if we came in and talked for a bit?" Kein asked.

"Yes, of course, Father. Come on in." Kathy opened the door all the way and moved aside.

"This is my friend Darby. She's here from Texas."

"Nice to meet you," Darby said as she shook Kathy's hand.

"Yes, ma'am. Nice to meet you as well." Kathy closed the door behind them and led them to the living room.

"Kathy, we need to ask some questions, if you don't mind," Kein started.

"Father, I'm sorry. Would you like a cup of coffee or tea before we start?" Kathy asked.

"Um, no thank you. I think we'll just go ahead and—"

"I'd like a cup of coffee if you have some made already," Darby cut in.

Kein glared at her as Kathy made her way to the kitchen.

"What? I'm thirsty. She offered first," Darby said sarcastically.

Kathy returned to the pair. "Here you are. Now, what can I help you all with?" she asked as she handed the cup to Darby and sat down with her daughter.

"Kathy, have you noticed any changes in Eli lately? Like mood swings or lashing out at people?" Kein asked.

"No. What is this about? Has Eli done something?"

"No ma'am, it's not that. We are just concerned about how he's doing. I know it affected him when your husband passed away, and we just want to make sure he's doing well and let him know that we are here for anything he may want to talk about. You haven't noticed him changing his eating habits or anything like that?" Laimend pressed on.

"No, not really. Though he did miss fried chicken day yesterday and then—well—I don't know if he ate last night either. Let me get him; he's in his room." Kathy stood up.

"No, just a second. Can we finish first, if that's ok?" Kein asked.

"Yes, of course." Kathy sat back down.

"So, minor eating changes. Any different clothing or a sudden interest in new music?" Laimend asked.

"No, not that I know of. But I spend a lot of my time in the café, Father. I don't know where he would have gotten money to get new clothes, though. He spends a lot of time in his room lately, but I think he's really trying to get some studying done in there. He's worried about college already. He's a good kid, Father." Kathy was starting to get a little worried now.

"I'm quite sure I would agree with you, Kathy. But even good people get on the wrong path from time to time. Yes, I think if it's OK with you, can we talk with Eli now?" Laimend asked.

"Yes, of course, Father. Let me get him," Kathy said as she stood up and turned around—only to see Eli standing in the hallway, staring at everyone.

"Oh, Eli, I was just going to get you. Father Laimend is here, and he would like to talk to you, if that's ok."

Eli stared at Laimend, and a smile crept over his face. The voice that came from his slender frame was not his own; it was deep, dark, and growling.

"You don't belong here, Father. You need to leave now. I don't want you here."

Kein recognized the voice. It was the voice from the thorn bush in his visions—deep and penetrating. Kein felt his ribs vibrate as the voice spoke.

"Your services are not needed here, Father. *Deus non est hic.*" He spoke in Latin.

"ELI, WHAT ARE YOU SAYING?" Kathy began, but Kein cut her off.

"That's Latin, Kathy. Very good, Eli. But you and I both know God is everywhere."

Darby asked, "What did he say?"

"He said God is not here," Laimend stated, never breaking eye contact with Eli. "Why don't you come sit and talk with us, then, if you have no reason to worry, Eli?"

"Father, I don't think that's Eli," Darby said.

"You are correct, but I need to continue to use his name until it's time not to. I need you to get them out of here, Darby. Take them to Charlene's or somewhere else," Kein said.

"I'm not leaving you here by yourself."

"It's fine. I will be fine. Just get them out of here, please, Darby. Don't argue."

Darby reluctantly grabbed Kathy by the arm and began to drag her out of the house with Mary. Suddenly, Eli's voice cried out, "Mother, don't leave me here with him. I'm scared."

"Eli," Kathy called out, struggling to break Darby's grasp. "Eli, hold on, I'll be right back."

"Kathy, that's not Eli," Kein said, and then the door closed.

"Come on over and have a seat. Let's talk about what happened to Eli."

The boy sat across from Laimend and smiled at him.

"So, what's your name, demon?"

"Ha ha ha ha. You think I'm just going to spill the beans, Father?" The deep voice came back. "I don't think you need to know that. All you need to know is I'm here to stay. Eli wants me here, and all of that stuff you've been finding has weakened you. Oh, and that little bump on your head? That will be your undoing. Might wanna get that looked at, Father. Ha ha ha."

The demon laughed and spit on the floor. It sizzled into the wood.

"So, tell me, demon. You say God isn't here—then why am I here? I represent God. Christ works through me. You know that."

Then Eli stood up and said, "You bore me, priest. I no longer desire this conversation."

He turned and walked back to his room, closing the door. Kein could hear chanting from the room. He pulled out his phone and called Darby quickly.

When she answered, he said, “Darby, I need you to go to my house and get my little black bag under my bed. Hurry. Break the window to get in.”

He hung up.

He made his way slowly down the hallway, trying to hear what was being said from Eli’s room. It was a continuous chant. He couldn’t make it out, but whatever it was, it wasn’t good. He tried the doorknob, but it was locked.

“What is the next move?” he said quietly to himself.

He stepped back into the living room, pulled out his phone and scrolled down to the number he was looking for. He stopped on Father O’Mally, opened the contact, and as he reached his thumb for the send button, his phone flew across the room and slammed into the wall.

He looked up and saw Eli standing in the hallway, staring at him.

“Ah ah ahhhh. No calling for backup, Father. It’s just you, your little slut friend, and me on the chessboard today. Your move.” The voice was slow and methodical.

“Alright then. What is your purpose? What’s your goal here?” Kein asked.

“Let’s wait for your friend to show up with the little bag of tricks, shall we? I don’t want to have to repeat myself for her when she gets here,” the voice said.

“So, are we just supposed to stand here and stare at each other?”

“Perhaps.”

“Don’t you have something to finish in Eli’s room?”

“Perhaps.”

“So, I can safely assume that you aren’t going to be cooperative, I guess,” Kein said with confidence.

“Ha ha ha ha......” The demon laughed, then sighed. “You just need to worry about keeping that wretched soup in your belly.”

Kein thought to himself, *He’s reading my mind.* He was feeling some acid reflux from the soup Charlene had prepared.

“How did you know that, demon?”

“I know all, priest. I’m the one you were told to be afraid of at night. I’m the one who was under your bed, waiting for you to fall asleep. Oh, young Kein—he was so afraid of the dark.”

His words came quickly now.

“AND FOR GOOD REASON. I WAS THERE!”

Just then, the door opened and Darby walked in without the bag.

“Darby, where is it? Where is the bag?”

“I sent Charlene to get it. She said she knew that house inside out,” Darby shot back.

“She isn’t going to be able to break the window, Darby!” Kein said, concerned now.

“Oh, she said she had a few spare keys to your house that she had made, just in case. I figured it would be ok.”

Kein rolled his eyes and turned back to Eli.

The demon laughed. “This will be fun. Me, you, the slut, and the old bitchy one.”

“She won’t be coming in here, and Darby will be leaving soon,” Kein responded.

“No, I’ll be staying, thank you very much,” Darby said. “Just tell me what to do.”

Kein whispered, “We need to sit him down and hold him there. Look for some rope or something.”

He turned back to the demon.

“I know you know what’s in my mind, but I promise you, you’re not strong enough to stop Jesus working through me. Eli, Eli, I need you to come out and help us a little bit.”

The demon let out a laugh.

“Eli, come on out here and help us. We need you to remember your time with the Church. You were an altar boy. You know Jesus.”

“SHUT IT, PRIEST.”

“Eli, Eli, I’m calling you out here. I need you to remember Jesus Christ is your savior, and He loves you. Come on, Eli.”

Just then, Darby moved behind Eli from the kitchen and wrapped her arms around him. She had some twine, the kind you tie up a turkey with.

“I’VE GOT HIM, FATHER!”

"YOU DON'T HAVE ANYTHING. YOU DON'T EVEN HAVE JESUS WITH YOU!" the demon snarled through the struggle.

Kein ran to her side and grabbed him from the front, but the demon slipped an arm free and elbowed Darby in the stomach. She fell, doubled over, shocked by the strength.

"YOU WILL NOT HOLD ME, PRIEST!"

They fell to the ground, Kein maintaining his bear-hug hold on the boy's body, but it was getting the better of him. The demon took his free hand and struck Father Kein in the head.

Laimend's head instantly erupted with shockwaves, like ripples in water—wave after wave of pain. His eyes closed, and he felt himself slipping away. Kein summoned all of his strength just to open them again.

Rolling on top of Father Laimend, the demon had the upper hand. He laughed and swung at Kein's head again.

"THAT'S ENOUGH."

The voice boomed from the front door, and heavy feet ran across the room. Kein heard the body dive across him and tackle the demon to the ground. He heard the struggle continue. A chair slid. Darby's voice shouted, "GOT HIM!" "HOLD THIS!"

Then another voice yelled, "TIGHTLY NOW, TIE IT TIGHT!" "THAT'S IT—NOW GET KEIN!"

And then he was out.

Chapter 8

Summoned

Laimend saw the lamb wound up in the thorns. It was now completely red from the blood pouring from its wounds. The thorns were tight against its legs, and every move it made caused more blood to cover the ground. It was crying out for help and kicking as Kein pulled at the bush. One vine came free, but two more grew around it. The lamb's face was barely visible anymore.

Kein looked around, but the shepherd was no longer there—only his staff, leaning against the side of the cliff. Kein grabbed it and, against the wind, made his way back to the lamb. He tried to pry the thorny vines away, but to no avail. The lamb's struggle became Kein's as he pulled and pried. The more he tugged at the vines, the tighter they became. It was as though they had a mind of their own. They knew what he was going to try next before he did. His hands were covered in the lamb's blood, causing them to slip.

Tears streamed down his face as he felt the pain of the animal. His own hands were torn and punctured from the thorns. There was blood everywhere. Kein fell back from exhaustion, sitting on his heels, his face drenched from crying, his hands and arms covered in blood from both he and the lamb.

Laimend got up on his knees and began to pray. "Lord, help me. Lord, this lamb's struggle is mine, and I give them both to you. Give me strength so that I may know what to do. Guide my hands through the thorns to save this animal. Lord God, send me Michael your Archangel to defend us in battle. Jesus, I plead with you to save this animal from the grasp of evil. Where thou art, there too is grace and mercy. Please, Lord, be with us here now."

As Laimend continued praying, a light began to shine from the shepherd's staff. It was so bright it began to light the entire cliff. It became blinding, with blue and white hues. Kein raised his arms to cover his eyes as the staff began to change form. It morphed and transformed into a sword right in front of him, then the light faded.

Kein picked up the sword by its hilt. It was heavy and light at the same time. The hilt fit in his hand perfectly. He lifted it in front of his face, and it spoke to him, saying, “The Lord is my shepherd; thou shalt not want. The shadow of death lives in the valley, but trust that something greater than the shadow of death is here, on the mountain with you.”

Kein stood up with the sword, and he could hear the voice of Rozas in the darkness, shouting his name.

“Kein, Kein, come on, my friend, we need you back here. Kein, wake up.”

Laimend looked down at the lamb in the thorns. He took a step toward it and then was blown off the cliff by the force of a huge wind, dropping the sword at the thorn bush. He heard laughter coming from the bush as he plunged deeper into the darkness.

Kein opened his eyes, and he could feel a wet rag on his head. Rozas was sitting next to him on the floor.

“He’s back,” Rozas shouted across the room. “Kein, are you ok, my friend?”

“Yes, yeah, I’m ok.” Kein sat up. Darby had obviously been crying. “Are you ok, Darby?”

“Yes, Father, I’m fine. This is just a lot to take in,” Darby said as she came to his side.

“Rozas, I didn’t know you were coming,” Laimend said to his friend, observing his bearded face.

"I told Darby not to tell you; it would only make you tell me not to, again. Ha. But I see you found what you were looking for here."

"Yes, yes I did," Kein said as he began to sit up with Rozas' help. "What happened?"

"You lost yourself in the thorns again," the dark voice came from across the room. "I know where you've been going, priest. Ha ha ha. You think you've been keeping it to yourself, but I know everything."

Kein looked at the body of Eli, sitting in a chair, his arms and legs tied down with rope and belts.

"You couldn't free the lamb, could you, priest? Ha ha ha."

The laughter was exactly like the one in Kein's visions.

Rozas said, "He hit you on the head and knocked you out. What is he talking about, my friend? Thorns? Lamb?"

"I'll fill you in later," Kein replied as he rose to his feet. "How long was I out?"

"About half an hour, Father," Darby chimed in.

Just then, there was a knock at the door. Rozas headed that way first, followed by Kein.

"The old hag is here, I see," Eli's body said in laughter.

Opening the door, Kein was greeted by Charlene.

"Here's your bag, Father. I know I wasn't supposed to have a key anymore—the one you took back, I mean—but I kept another. I didn't tell you."

She was fumbling with the key in her hand, unable to meet his eyes.

"I know I shouldn't have done it. I just... I was scared something would happen to you, and I didn't know what else to do."

Kein smiled and gave her the biggest hug. "Mrs. Baker, I have never been happier to find out that you had a key to my house." He took the bag from her hands. "You hang on to that key, Charlene. I think it's a great idea that you have the spare." A huge smile crept over Charlen's face.

"Hey, Mrs. Baker, help me, please," Eli's voice came from inside the home.

"What? What's going on in there?" Charlene asked, trying to get inside. As she shoved her way through the door, she saw Eli tied to the chair, struggling and ran to him. "Oh my God, what are you doing to him?"

"Charlene, stop. It's not him. That's not Eli," Kein shouted.

Darby jumped to grab her and pull her back by the shoulders, but it was too late. That deep laughter came from Eli's body, and then he spat into Charlene's eyes.

"Oh! Oh, what is this? Oh, it burns my eyes!" Charlene shouted, wiping at her face.

Kein rushed to grab a towel and helped her clean her face.

"Charlene, Eli is possessed. There's something in him that we have to get out. I need you to go and take care of Kathy and Mary now. Make sure they are OK and that they don't come back here until we say it's ok."

"Oh my God, are you serious? Here in Redmond?" She was shocked and terrified, but surprisingly in control of her emotions. "Yes, yes, of course, Father. I'll—I'll do that. Yes."

Charlene stammered as she made her way to the front door. Rozas shut the door behind her, and Kein opened his black bag and pulled out a bottle, a crucifix, and some oils and salts.

"Let's begin," he said to Rozas.

"I've never performed an exorcism, only witnessed one, so I don't know how much help I'll be, Kein," Rozas said.

"It's fine. Let's go and get cleansed. I need to confess, and so do you—and you too, Darby," Kein said as he turned to her.

She nodded in confirmation, and Kein led her to the kitchen, where she confessed and he absolved her. He explained that sins that are forgiven are blocked from the view of the demon; they are covered in the blood of Christ now. He anointed her and then called over Rozas. They exchanged confessions and were cleansed.

Then Kein turned to Eli. Drool was dripping from his chin, and his eyes were completely red except for his pupils. There was visible thinning of the skin, and Kein could see the veins in his face now. This was progressing quickly.

"What is your name, demon?" Kein asked calmly, as Darby and Rozas stood on either side of the chair, just behind Eli's visible spit radius. "Tell me, why are you in this boy?"

"Ha ha ha. So polite, so proper in asking. Go screw yourself, priest." The demon spoke in the same tone as Laimend, mocking him.

"In the name of Jesus Christ, I demand you tell me your name."

"Christ Jesus of name the in... How about... no... ha ha ha."

The laughter was deeper and felt like the walls of the house had to expand to contain it. Kein felt it vibrating in his ribs. It was speaking backwards as a mockery, this was a bad sign. This was something strong.

Laimend started, "I said—" then the boy's body lifted forward from the chair, his arms and legs still bound to it. His entire midsection lifted, and then the chair began to rise from the floor. There was a screech, and then loud screaming came from Eli's body.

The boy's face was staring straight at Father Laimend. His eyes went ghost white in an instant.

"GRAB HIM! HOLD HIM TO THE FLOOR!" Kein shouted to Rozas and Darby.

They each grabbed a side and could barely pull the chair back down to the ground. The room filled with noise coming from the boy, and the sound of wind filled the whole house.

"THIS IS NOT WORKING, FATHER!" Rozas shouted over the inhuman noise coming from the boy.

"WE NEED A CLEAN SPACE!"

"WHAT DO YOU MEAN, A CLEAN SPACE?" Darby shouted back.

They pulled the chair fully to the ground, and the screaming slowly faltered to nothing. Eli was staring at Kein, not flinching, not blinking, just staring and drooling, his eyes crystal white.

"He means we need to bring him to the Cathedral," Kein said, almost defeated, knowing how difficult it would be to move him if he decided to act out once untied. "Darby, go get Rozas' car and bring it around front."

"Father, how are we—"

Kein cut her off. "Just go get it, please."

Darby got the keys from Rozas and took off out the door. It was an hour before dark. *Probably better to move him when no one would be outside watching*, Kein thought, but they would have to make do with the time constraints.

"My friend, we need to contain him better before we untie him from the chair," Rozas said.

"No need," Kein started. "We will move him with minimal fight. I've seen this look before. It's gone back inside, building power right now. We have a small window to get him moved to the Cathedral before he comes back full force."

"Father, are you sure?"

"Yes, I'm sure. We can stand him, tie him, and walk him to the car," Kein said.

The two men untied Eli's arms and legs and stood him up. Nothing—only the blank stare from the white eyes. Eli's gaze followed Kein wherever he went, never breaking his view of Laimend. They tied his hands together at the wrists and led him to the front door.

"Father, it's still early. Should we wait for a bit?" Rozas asked, worried about the neighbors seeing what was going on.

"We don't have that kind of time, I'm afraid," Kein responded.

They opened the front door and led Eli down the steps to the waiting car. Kathy's neighbor was outside and waved to Father Laimend. He waved back, trying to be normal, but she took this as a sign to come say hello.

"Get him in the car, Rozas," Kein said.

"Hello, Mrs. Bradford. How are you today?" Kein stepped in, cutting her off from seeing Eli.

"Oh, it's just been a wonderful day, albeit a bit cold. How about you, Father? Whatcha doing at Kathy's?" she responded.

"Oh, it's been just a great few days lately. I was able to spend some time with some old friends, but we were just stopping in to check on things and make sure everyone is doing well at Kathy's," Kein said, trying to maneuver his way out of the conversation.

"Well, introduce me to your friend and the other priest. I would love to tell them how wonderful you are, Father," Mrs. Bradford said with a smile.

"Well, uh, we actually need to get going to the Cathedral, but maybe next time. Would that be ok?" Kein said, slowly backing away toward the car.

"Well, now don't be silly. This'll only take a second," she said as she walked past Kein toward the car.

Rozas turned around as he closed the back seat door and saw the woman approaching.

"Well, good afternoon. My name is Monseigneur Rozas. How are you doing this wonderful afternoon?"

"Well, see, now that's hospitality," Mrs. Bradford said sarcastically, looking back at Kein. "I'm fine, thank you. My name is Mrs. Bradford, and I just want to tell you how wonderful Father Laimend is. He is just a blessing here in Redmond. Since he took over St. Augustine's, we have all just felt the presence of God in this town. And who's your friend over there?" she asked, pointing at the driver's seat of the car where Darby was sitting.

"Oh, that is a friend of mine from Texas," Kein chimed in. "Darby—Darby, would you come meet one of my wonderful parishioners, Mrs. Bradford?"

Darby leaned out of the passenger window and waved with a smile. "It's so nice to meet you. Father, I hate to rush you, but I think bedtime is almost over."

"Ah yes, it was wonderful to meet you," Rozas said as he quickly walked to the car and slid in behind the driver's seat.

"Mrs. Bradford, we will talk again soon. Have a great evening," Kein said as he backed away toward the car door. He slid into the passenger seat, shut the door, and buckled his seatbelt.

Inside, Eli was beginning to growl. He was huffing, his nostrils flaring wildly, and he was staring at Kein with those white eyes. A smile had replaced the blank stare on his face.

"Drive," Laimend said to Darby.

She put the car in drive and took off toward the Cathedral.

Sliding to a stop in front of the Cathedral, the massive cross atop the steeple stared down at the car, as though Jesus Christ himself was waiting for the showdown about to commence. Kein and Rozas were practically carrying Eli through the front doors. His feet dragged, scraping the threshold as they crossed it.

Darby shut the doors behind them and followed to the Sacristy in the back of the Cathedral, where they set him down in a chair and restrained him before he could come back to reality. The smile on his face was completely without feeling—just pure evil looking at Kein from somewhere behind Eli's eyes.

"Can you do this, my friend?" Rozas asked.

"I can, yes," Kein began. "Lord God, you are with us in this holy place, and you have the power to drive out this demon from Eli. Pray with me," he said to Rozas and Darby. "Our Father, who art in heaven, hallowed be thy name, thy kingdom—"

They continued praying until the moment Eli spoke in his own voice.

"Father... Father Kein? What—what's going on?"

"Did it work?" Darby asked.

Rozas responded, "No. That's the demon hiding behind him. It is waiting, trying not to be ejected from the host."

"Eli," Kein started, "Eli, I need you to tell me what you did. I need to know what you've been doing to allow this thing inside of you."

"Nothing, Father. Nothing."

"Eli, this is not the time to worry about getting in trouble. You need to tell me—"

The dark voice took over. "He's mine. He accepted a covenant with me."

"WHAT IS YOUR NAME, DEMON?" Kein shouted and touched Eli's head with anointing oil. He felt heat radiating from the boy's skin.

The demon shrieked, “AHHH! THE FOUL STENCH FROM YOUR DEAD BODY WILL FILL THE WHOLE TOWN!”

“In the name of Jesus Christ our Lord—the one who died for our sins, the one who commands you and all—tell me your name, demon.”

“I OWE YOU NOTHING, PRIEST!” the demon shouted. The voices of Rozas and Darby praying the rosary in the background overwhelmed the demon’s protests. “AND THESE ONES—THEY ARE NOTHING TO ME.”

Darby spoke out. “Tell us your name, demon. Jesus Christ commands you.”

Before Kein could stop her, the demon turned its head almost completely around, looked directly at Darby, and spoke calmly, calculating every word.

“Jesus I know. You, I know not. You command nothing. Ha ha ha.”

“Darby, don’t speak to it at all. Not a single word,” Laimend said harshly. “It will use everything against you.”

Then the demon spoke again to Darby.

“You are only a piece of meat to us. We use you for what we need and then dispose of you when your flesh is stinking and rotting. You are nothing—beneath us, little girl. We do as we please with you.”

Laimend took charge again. “THAT’S ENOUGH! You’re talking to God through me, demon. Now tell me your name.”

The demon turned its head back toward Kein.

“I am the one who is called upon.”

“Your name, demon. The blood of Christ is in this place. Tell me your name.”

“I am the one who helps those who ask for it.”

“THE POWER OF CHRIST COMPELS YOU. WHAT IS YOUR NAME?”

“I AM HE WHO COMES TO THOSE WHO WISH TO USE ME.”

“YOUR NAME! GOD ALMIGHTY IS IN THIS PLACE. JESUS CHRIST IS IN THIS PLACE. THE HOLY SPIRIT IS IN THIS PLACE. YOU WILL TELL ME YOUR NAME!”

“I AM HE, THE BRINGER OF MANIFESTATION, THE ONE LILITH SENDS. I AM SAM’AEL!”

The demon shouted. Kein could see Eli’s vocal cords pressing against his skin. The boy was in pain.

Kein stepped back. “Sam’ael… Sam’ael. Why is that name familiar?” he said to himself.

“Hold him. Keep praying and do not engage in conversation,” Kein ordered as he ran to the reliquary, where the relics were held. He knew he had not learned them all yet. St. Augustine had quite a few, but he didn’t know which one he needed.

Kein stumbled through the pages of the list of items. He looked at everything in it. He could hear the demon laughing from the back of the Cathedral. His hands were shaking, and he was losing belief in himself.

He hurried to his black bag at the front of the Cathedral. Darby had dropped it there on her way in. Inside, he pulled out a thick book, opened it, found the section on the letter S, and then found the name Sam'ael.

Sam'ael: "Frequently named as Lilith's consort. He is known as the Slant Serpent, while Lilith is the Tortuous Serpent. In the Kabbalistic texts, considered one of the rulers of the dark side next to Lilith. Sam'ael represents the malevolent force. They are the ones who are behind witchcraft and manifestation."

"Oh my God... witchcraft!" Kein shouted to himself. "Those friends and Eli were playing in witchcraft. I knew it. That new age store sells those books. What were they thinking!"

Kein grabbed his phone and dialed the number.

"It's time to call in some backup," he said to himself.

Chapter 9

The Cost of Invocation

"Ah now, Father Laimend. How goes it in the States, my friend?"

"Not good, Father O'Malley. I need your help." Kein's voice was exasperated. He explained the situation to Father O'Malley in Ireland from across the world. It was fast-paced, and Laimend couldn't slow his speech down.

"Son, ya need ta calm down. The demon'll always have the upper hand until ya take control. Don't let it get to ya. You're the one it's afraid of, not the other way round." O'Malley's words were comforting to hear. "Now then, let's see..." Kein could hear O'Malley shuffling pages of a book. "So, Sam'ael is there representin' witchcraft. I don't see a specific relic that Sam'ael runs from, but Saint Benedict is the patron saint against all evils, devils, and witchcraft, lad. I think we start there."

"YES, THAT'S RIGHT! GREAT POINT, FATHER!" Kein responded, now overly excited to be seeing some headway.

"Now go have a look an' see if ya've got any fancy relic from Benedict," O'Malley said. Kein took his phone and went to the reliquary, skimming through the list until he found it.

"WE HAVE A PIECE OF HIS THIGH BONE HERE, FATHER!" Kein was ecstatic.

"That's grand, lad. Grab it and let's get started," O'Malley said.

"Let's? Father O'Malley, I can't wait for you to get here for this." Kein was confused.

"No, lad. Keep me on the phone. Put up the camera and let me help through the phone. The evil ones use electronics ta manipulate people. I figure we can use electronics ta work against 'em, eh?" O'Malley responded.

"Yes, Father, we definitely can." Kein set down his phone and began trying to locate the relic.

Back in the Sacristy, Darby and Rozas continued praying the Rosary nonstop. When it was finished, they would begin again—first the Joyful, then the Sorrowful, then the Glorious mysteries. Rozas led each decade and Darby followed. "Hail Mary, full of grace..."

The demon was very agitated now, struggling to break the bonds to the chair. Darby could see its power was restrained here in the Cathedral. It struggled physically but could not exert power outside the body. Though still strong, it stretched the ropes, and Darby could hear the wood creaking on the chair arms. It was not able to levitate the chair as it had done at Kathy's home. This seemed like good news to Darby. She continued praying with Rozas. It was the only thing she knew she could do for sure.

Kein came rushing in with his phone in one hand and a small box in the other. "Give me one more moment, please," he said, rushing back out of the room and leaving the box on a desk. "Father O'Malley, do you wish to confess anything today?"

"Yes, I do, Father," O'Malley began. Back in the Sacristy, Rozas kept an eye on Eli, watching his reaction to the box Kein had brought in.

"What is that? GET IT AWAY FROM ME!" the deep voice shouted. "THAT OLD SACK OF MEAT WASN'T WORTH THE CAVE HE LIVED IN!"

Darby shuddered at the shouting. It felt as though each word passed through her body like water. She didn't understand what was happening, but Rozas did. He prayed intently, watching Eli's body convulse every time his eyes landed on the box. He didn't know what was inside it, but he knew it was powerful—powerful enough to terrify this demon.

After the confession, Kein walked back in with Father O'Malley on video chat and set up his phone so everyone could see—and so O'Malley could see Eli.

"This one's yours, lad. We're all behind ya, son," O'Malley said to Laimend.

Kein began, "Sam'ael, granter of wishes and witchcrafts, you're nothing more than a fake genie, and you don't belong here. You know that. Now, Jesus Christ commands you to leave this body, leave this place, and return to the Hell from whence you came."

"I do not take commands from you, priest."

"No, but you do take commands from Christ. He lives in me, works through me, and He is the one removing you from this body," Kein responded.

"I was asked to be here. I entered into a covenant with the boy, and I will not leave. This one is mine. He wants me here."

"You are not authorized to stay, foul thing. You have run out of time here." Kein could hear O'Malley's prayers behind him, Rozas and Darby in front of him, and he felt the Holy Spirit enter the room. "Be gone, demon. This is the command of God. Go back to your place of darkness!"

"SCREW YOU, PRIEST! THIS IS MY SUIT TO WEAR, MY BAG OF BONES—AND YOU CAN GO BACK WHERE YOU CAME FROM, AND YOU TOO, DRUNK MURDERER!"

Kein faltered. The words struck him hard.

"OH, SHUT YER MOUTH, BEAST, AND LET THE MAN DO HIS JOB!" O'Malley roared through the phone.

That gave Kein a surge of confidence, and he reached for the box.

"DON'T! STOP IT! KEEP HIM AWAY FROM ME!"

The demon began to thrash violently. Rozas and Darby grabbed Eli as the screaming filled the room, wind rushing through the space. Darby saw one rope snap, then another, the sound cracking like gunshots.

"KEEP PRAYING!" Rozas shouted.

"OUR FATHER, WHO ART IN HEAVEN—" They were screaming the Lord's Prayer now.

Kein opened the box and removed the bone fragment. He held it up. "YOU KNOW WHAT THIS IS?"

"KEEP HIM AWAY FROM ME, YOU PIECE OF SHIT! NO—NO—STOP IT!"

The chair snapped backward. Eli's leg tore free and slammed into Laimend's head.

Darkness. White noise. Kein felt the floor strike his shoulder. He heard the bone fragment hit the ground with a sharp crack.

"FATHER KEIN!"

"DON'T YA WORRY 'BOUT HIM—GRAB THE RELIC, DARBY!"

"GET OFF ME! DON'T TOUCH ME, WHORE!"

"PUT IT TO HIS HEAD!"

"NOW, DARBY! HOLD IT TO HIS HEAD!" O'Malley commanded between prayers.
"GOOD LASS! KEEP IT THERE! GLORY BE TO THE FATHER, AND TO THE SON, AND TO THE HOLY SPIRIT—"

Kein felt himself fading. This was it. But he pulled strength from God and forced his eyes open. He saw Rozas struggling to keep Eli pinned, Darby fighting to hold the relic to his head.

"FATHER! GIVE ME THE STRENGTH TO FINISH THIS!"

A force grabbed Kein at the waist and pulled him to his knees. He looked down and saw the hand of Christ holding him. Jesus stood before him, smiling, lifting him one step at a time toward Eli.

"FATHER KEIN, YA CAN DO THIS, LAD!" O'Malley shouted, he could see Laimend being led by Christ.

Laimend placed his hand on Darby, pulling her out of her focus. She turned, and he smiled at her with complete peace. She could feel something different. She placed the bone fragment in his hand and stepped aside.

"DARBY, NOW! I'VE GOT HIM—DO IT NOW!" Rozas shouted.

Laimend knelt beside Rozas, met his eyes, and smiled.

The struggle stopped.

The demon was no longer fighting.

Father Laimend placed his hand on his friend's shoulder, steady and sure, and in that touch Rozas felt something settle inside him. He knew—without question—that everything was going to be all right. Father O'Malley could see the glowing figure standing beside Kein, though no one else could. He knew, with a reverence that left him trembling, that Jesus Himself was there. O'Malley prayed without pause, prayer after prayer spilling from his lips, even when words failed him entirely.

Kein turned toward Eli's body—and toward the thing that had wrapped itself around the boy's grief. Terror seized Eli's face, his features twisting as though something within him was being torn open. It was not rage that contorted him now. It was the unbearable pain of being seen.

The demon tried to pull Eli backward, scrambling desperately, but there was nowhere left to retreat. The wall pressed against his back, cold and final. Father Laimend stepped closer. Blood welled from Eli's fingertips as he clawed at the marble floor, nails breaking, leaving red streaks behind him—each scrape a plea to escape what love had cornered.

Kein lifted his right hand and pressed it gently to Eli's forehead. The relic of St. Benedict rested in his palm. When he spoke, his voice was not his own.

"Eli... hey, buddy."

The boy's body shuddered.

"I know," the voice continued softly. "I know you're hurting. I know losing me felt like the world ended. I know you just wanted to hear my voice again. I would've done the same thing, son. I would've done anything to see you."

Kein's eyes filled, though his voice remained steady.

"This thing told you it could help. It lied to you. It used how much you love me. But listen to me now—I'm okay. I'm not lost.

I'm not gone. I'm with God, Eli. I'm at peace. And I never stopped loving you. Not for a second."

A faint hint of color began to return to Eli's eyes, the white slowly retreating.

"Eli," the voice said gently. "You don't need this anymore. You don't need to hurt to hold on to me. I'm still your dad. And I'm right here."

Eli's body convulsed violently. Darby fell to her knees, sobbing, praying through tears she couldn't stop. She didn't understand what she was witnessing—only that something sacred and terrible was unfolding before her, and it broke her open.

Rozas stood frozen, overwhelmed by the force pouring through Kein. In that moment, he understood why Father Kein Laimend had been spared, why he had been chosen. Rozas folded his hands and looked to Heaven—not praying for the boy, but begging God to hold Kein once this was over.

"Eli," the voice said again, quieter now. "I need you to tell me something. I need to know you remember who loves you more than even I do. I need you to tell me you know Jesus loves you."

Eli's body convulsed harder. Black foam spilled from his mouth. He didn't answer.

"Eli, son," the voice broke. "I miss you so much. Every day. But I need you to let go. I need you to choose life. Choose Him. For me."

"I..." Eli's voice cracked. Tears streamed down his face, cutting through the grime. "I..."

"You can do this," the voice whispered. "I'm so proud of you. I always have been."

"I... know..."

"Jesus loves you, Eli. He's been with you even when I couldn't be. Trust Him."

"I... know... Jesus... loves me."

"Yes," the voice said, trembling. "Yes, He does. Can you tell me who your Lord and Savior is?"

"Jesus is."

"I need you to say it, son. Say it all the way."

The bone fragment burned against Eli's skin. Smoke rose. The black foam hissed as it hit the floor.

"Jesus... Christ... is my Lord," Eli sobbed. "Jesus Christ is my Lord... and Savior."

"One more time, buddy," the voice pleaded. "Say it for me."

"JESUS CHRIST IS MY LORD AND SAVIOR!"

"I love you," the voice said softly. "I always will. I'll be waiting for you."

Eli's eyes snapped fully back to their natural color. A scream tore out of him—not in terror, but release—as something ancient was ripped away. His head fell back against the wall, his body going limp. Smoke and black foam spilled from his mouth and burned the marble floor.

Eli's eyes closed.

And for the first time in a long while, his face was at peace.

Kein turned around and looked at Father O'Malley through the phone. Jesus spoke through him, saying, "My son, you have been forgiven of your sins of the past. You can forgive yourself now."

O'Malley smiled through a tear and nodded back at Jesus.

Then Kein looked over at Jesus and tried to talk, but he couldn't. Jesus smiled at him and set him on the floor, laid him down, and then let go. Kein watched as Jesus lifted into the air and faded from view. Then his eyes closed.

He could hear the scrambling of feet, furniture moving, scraping the floor. He could hear Darby's voice. "Father, wake up. Father Kein." He heard the voice of Rozas. "Yes, we need an ambulance, please. The address is—"

Kein felt complete peace. His head no longer hurt; the throbbing had subsided. He was thankful for that. He felt so much gratitude to God for helping him, allowing him to do this, to help Eli.

Kein could hear Father O'Malley on the phone, trying to calm the others. "The boy is movin'. Check on him now and make sure he's all right. Call his mother and let her know..."

Kein was grateful for having O'Malley to help him end this dark magic.

Then the noise slowly faded away.

Nothing now.

Just darkness.

Kein opened his eyes. He was lying on the rocks of the cliff. A bit away, he saw the lamb, still covered in blood and intertwined in the thorns. His nerves were calm. He could see the blood all over his hands, still oozing from the wounds the thorns had imposed on him.

Laimend stood up slowly, taking in all of his surroundings. He looked around at the darkness over the cliff's edge. Taking a step back from it, he turned and saw the shepherd standing near the entrance to the passageway they had originally passed through. Kein looked back at the lamb and then to the shepherd. He nodded in understanding.

Slowly, Father Kein walked toward the sword that lay on the ground near the thorn bush. Wrapping his hand around the hilt felt natural, as though this sword was made for his hand. The grooves in the metal fit perfectly into his fingers. In this moment, he and the sword were one.

Kein stepped to the bush and swung at it. Instantly, the piece he cut off withered and died on the ground at his feet. He could hear screams from the bush, but they were coming from the darkness beyond the cliff's edge. He swung again and again, cutting off piece by piece of the thorns. He grabbed the bush and pulled it away from the lamb's skin, watching as the blood stopped flowing from the puncture wounds.

Every thorn he removed from the lamb left a hole in its skin, and as he removed each piece, he watched as the hole closed on its own. The blood dripping from it went back into the wound as it closed—like a red waterfall moving upstream instead of down, each trail of blood retracting inside the lamb.

He slashed and cut and pulled away at the vines and thorns until there were no more wrapped around the lamb. He watched as the animal kicked and struggled to move out of the trap. Kein used the sword to dig at the ground, removing the roots from the rocky soil and pulling them away from the lamb's legs and hooves. Slowly, the lamb became free, able to move. It kicked with Kein, removing the underbrush and intertwined vines.

When he removed the last piece of root from the ground, the lamb kicked one last time and jumped past Laimend. He watched from his knees as the lamb ran to the shepherd. The shepherd bent over and ran his hand across the lamb's face. True joy, absolute bliss, and peace overcame them both. Then the lamb looked back at Kein and took off through the passageway back to its flock.

Kein stood up, using the sword as leverage. He started kicking the roots and dead thorns over the edge of the cliff. Sounds of terror and horrible cries of torture came from below. As he kicked the last piece over the edge, it was as though the screams he heard were falling with it. They faded into the darkness, and the cries faded with them. Now silence prevailed—pure silence and peace.

Kein walked over to the shepherd and reached out to hand him the sword. In his hands, the sword morphed into the Word of God. They were absorbed into his skin, like when skin absorbs water. It flowed through his veins, and he could feel the Word throughout his whole body. In every fiber of his being—every cell, every ounce of blood—he carried the Word of God. He could feel it in his head, surrounding the tumor in his brain. It was painful, but peaceful at the same time.

He looked at the shepherd. He was holding his staff again. The shepherd looked at him and spoke to Father Laimend without opening his mouth; he spoke directly into Kein's head.

"Your work is done, Kein Laimend. Thank you for saving my lost lamb. Rejoice, for all of Heaven celebrates today."

Kein replied, "What now? What do I do now?"

"You need only follow me. Truly, I tell you, my yoke is easy."

"I will, my Lord. I have always tried to."

The voice said, "You always have been a good and faithful servant. I know you, and I love you. Your works here are done."

"Your will be done. I follow you, Lord," Kein replied.

"Then it is as it should be. All is well, Kein Laimend."

Then the voice went silent.

Kein watched as the shepherd turned and walked through the passageway. He stepped forward to follow him, but the rocks closed in on the passage. Kein tried to call out, but he couldn't speak; his voice was gone from him. He pushed at the rocks, but they wouldn't move.

Kein stepped back and felt a force from above. As he looked up, he saw light—pure light—and peace came with it. Kein closed his eyes and felt himself lifting from the ground. The warmth surrounded his body.

He knew this was an important moment.

Chapter 10

Between Heaven and Earth

Kein's eyes opened to the bright lights above his head. He heard beeping noises—machines, people talking. His head hurt, but not as badly as it had before. He tried to look around, but he couldn't move his neck; it was braced somehow.

He tried to talk, but there was a tube in his mouth. He was in a hospital. He could see his feet moving under the blanket. He could feel his fingers moving. In his line of vision, Rozas stood in the doorway talking to someone in scrubs. Kein couldn't make out what they were saying, but by the look on Rozas' face, it wasn't good. He looked confused, almost scared.

When the nurse noticed Kein's eyes open, she turned and walked out. Rozas stepped to the bedside and began praying. "Thank you, Lord God. You are the Almighty, creator of Heaven and Earth. May your will be done forever and ever. We thank you for sending Father Kein back to us. We thank you for allowing him to continue to serve you and us through you. Amen."

The doctor walked in with the nurse right behind her, Darby following close. "Father Laimend, you're in the hospital. Can you hear me? Blink twice if you can hear me."

Kein blinked twice.

"Okay, that's good. My name is Doctor Morgan. You took a nasty blow to the head. We're in Houston, Texas, and you're in good hands, okay?"

Kein blinked twice again.

"So, your CT scans from last year show a tumor in your brain. Do you remember that?"

Kein blinked twice.

"Good. Okay. We're going to give you something to help you rest, and we'll talk more tomorrow. I promise, you're going to be okay. Just get some rest for now, all right?"

Kein blinked twice again. He watched the nurse insert a needle into his IV and inject a clear liquid. Almost instantly, he felt himself fading away. The lights dimmed, the noises subsided, and he was out.

He found himself staring at the shepherd and his flock—all of them. Kein dropped to his knees and began giving thanks. For his role in helping people. For God's grace. For showing him the path he was meant for. He gave thanks and praise for everything. Then he heard the voice of God again.

"With you I am well pleased, you are welcomed in my home now. Who, then, will go forth in my name?"

Kein opened his mouth and cried out, "HERE I AM, SEND ME!" He remembered the verse from Isaiah 6:8. It was a moment of pure peace. Without hesitation, he knew he was the one to go forth, proclaiming the Kingdom, fulfilling the good works. And he knew his time was not now.

Then a great wind blew through the shepherd and his flock. Though they did not notice it, Kein felt it blow directly into his head, as though it were blowing inside his brain. The wind began to lift him, carrying him off the ground and into the sky. Then a blinding light came over him.

Kein opened his eyes and was back in the hospital bed, still hooked up to machines. He could hear the doctor talking to Rozas and Darby.

"We just don't understand it. It doesn't make sense. Two days ago, it was there and now it's not."

Rozas laughed. "Ha! Well, the Lord works in mysterious ways."

Doctor Morgan replied, "No offense, Father, but we don't live in miracle land here. There is a scientific explanation for everything that happens, and we need to be able to explain it."

"Well, good luck with that, Doctor," Darby chimed in. "With everything I've seen lately, there isn't always an explanation other than a miracle."

Doctor Morgan walked over to Kein. The hoses and tubes were removed from his mouth. He could talk a little now, though his throat was very dry and scratchy.

"Father Kein, I don't know what happened, but two days ago when you arrived, we took a scan of your brain and compared it to the imaging from your last visit. They matched. The tumor was still there–it was actually growing."

"Yes, I know it's there," Kein said, struggling to speak.

"Well, that's just it," the doctor replied. "It's not."

"What do you mean?" Kein asked, puzzled.

"The other day we immobilized you for fear of the tumor rupturing–it was that large," Doctor Morgan continued. "Yesterday, we prepped you for surgery. In the operating room, with a live scan, it showed nothing. We reran the previous scans and took another set of scans. It's not there, Father. It's not in your head anymore. What changed in one day?"

"You're the doctor," Kein said. "You tell me."

“Well, I don’t have an explanation yet. But you’re not leaving anytime soon. We have tests to run and results to wait on, so get comfortable, Father.”

The doctor stood and walked out.

“Father, it’s really good to see you doing better,” Darby said from the other side of the bed. She hugged him, then stood. “I’m going to head back to Williamstown. It’s been a bit too long of a vacation—and a bit too exciting. I’ll call you soon, Monseigneur Rozas, to check in, okay?”

“Of course, Darby. It was so good seeing you. I’ll call if anything changes.”

Darby walked out of the room and down the hall.

“That one’s in it for life now, Kein,” Rozas said, leaning closer. “She’s a good one to call on when we’re in need.”

“We?” Kein strained to say.

Rozas laughed. “Well, you keep getting sent places that need help. You can’t do it alone, so I assume I’ll be helping. And she did good this time.”

“I see,” Kein said. “And Eli—how is he?”

“He’s fine. Everything’s fine in Redmond. Father Pete is covering for you, and Charlene is taking care of your car and belongings. All is well, my friend. Just rest.”

Kein lay back and closed his eyes. He felt peace in everything that had happened over the past few months. He was completely at peace with the path God had set before him.

Two weeks passed. Kein was able to move around. He was eating better. His throat had healed, and his head was no longer a source of pain. The doctor signed off on restoring his license, and Kein was ready to return to St. Augustine's Cathedral and resume his post in Redmond.

"So, Father Kein, we still can't explain what happened with your tumor," Doctor Morgan said with a slight smile. "It's completely gone. Every scan shows no indication of it returning. I have to say, I'm baffled."

"I don't like not knowing things," the doctor continued. "This isn't in my wheelhouse. The not knowing makes me uncomfortable."

"Well, growth happens when you're uncomfortable, Doctor," Kein replied with a smile. "Maybe I'll see you at Mass one day."

"After this, I might have to," Doctor Morgan said. "Father Kein Laimend, it was nothing short of interesting meeting you. I'm glad you're doing well. Take care of yourself."

"I have Jesus taking care of me," Kein replied as he picked up his bag. "My job, like yours, is to take care of others—just in a different way."

Outside the hospital, Rozas waited in the car. Kein slid into the passenger seat.

"Take me home, Rozas—or at least to the airport."

They laughed the whole way.

As Kein walked away from his friend into the airport he shouted back, "keep the beard, it suits you."

This flight was different. Kein wasn't afraid. He knew he would land safely.

Charlene Baker waited at the arrival gate and wrapped him in the biggest hug. "Father Laimend, I was so relieved to hear you were okay. We were all so worried. Eli started a prayer group for you. That's all we did—pray."

"Really?" Kein smiled. "Eli started it?"

"Yes. And guess what? He's decided to join the Seminary next year. He felt the calling. Kathy is so proud of him."

"His dad is too, Charlene—his dad is too," Kein said, a tear trying to escape his eye as they walked out to the parking lot.

"Well, here, I suppose you will want to drive," Charlene said as she handed him the keys.

Kein looked up to see his beautiful white 1965 Ford Mustang sitting in the parking spot, shiny and clean, as though it had been waiting for him for years. The red leather interior had been cleaned and oiled so well it could have been on a showroom floor.

"Mrs. Baker, you didn't have to do that. I do appreciate it ever so much, though. Thank you," Kein said as he gave her another hug.

"Oh, I didn't. I hired Eli to do it. He wanted to do something nice for you, and I thought this was the best thing he could have done," she said.

"This is just great—really. I can't thank you enough, Charlene. You have been nothing but wonderful to me, and I appreciate it," Kein said as they got into the car.

"Father, did you know this thing can go from zero to sixty in about 5.2 seconds? I'm not saying I tried it, but I will say I believe it."

They both laughed as he pulled out of the parking lot.

The next day, Father Kein relieved Father Pete, and they exchanged the goings-on in town and at the Cathedral. Nothing major—mostly the usual. Father Pete mentioned he had tried to clean the spot in the Sacristy where there was a strange burn mark on the floor. Kein told him not to worry about it; it was a part of the Cathedral now. In the back of his mind, he knew it was from the black foam that had poured out of Eli's mouth. It had burned the marble floor, and that mark would remain forever.

Father Pete packed his belongings and left for his new parish.

That afternoon, Father Kein walked to the café to have supper and say hello to Kathy. When he walked in, Eli jumped up from the corner booth and wrapped his arms around him.

"Thank you for not giving up on me, Father," was all Eli could say. His tears said the rest.

Kathy came from behind the counter and hugged him next, thanking him for everything. "I'm so sorry I didn't know. I'm so sorry—I just didn't know he was doing that."

"It's okay, Kathy. Trust me, it's okay. He is fine, and everything is as it should be. You have a great young man here, and you are doing a wonderful job, Mom," Kein said. "Now, how are we in the way of fried chicken?" he added with a laugh.

"I'll have it right out, Father. Unsweet tea too?"

"You know, I think I'll indulge just this once. Could I have a sweet tea?" he asked.

“You sure can, Father. You can have whatever you want.”

Sitting down with Eli, Kein started the conversation. “So, how are your friends doing—Dillon and Doug?”

“Didn’t you hear? They moved, Father. It’s like they were never here. Nobody remembers seeing them except Mom and me. I really can’t explain it.”

“Really? How interesting,” Kein said, wondering if they had been sent to lead Eli astray, to guide him away from God. But they had attended Mass—how was that possible? Or had they? “Well, we will just have to trust in God’s plan for us all, Eli.”

“Yes, Father. I’m joining the Seminary—did you hear?”

“Yes, I did. That’s wonderful, Eli. I’m so proud of you for making such a bold decision. You’re going to do wonderful things in God’s name; I just know it. And if you need a letter of recommendation, give me a call. I can get you two letters in no time.”

“Really, Father? You would do that?”

“With the experience you have under your belt, absolutely.”

Just then, Kathy brought out a huge plate of fried chicken with all the sides. She set down a large glass of sweet tea in front of Father Laimend and stepped back.

“Well, gentlemen, will that be all?” Kathy asked with a grin.

“Yes, ma’am. Thank you very much,” Kein said.

She stood there staring at him, unnerving him a bit. “Is there something I’m missing, Kathy?”

"No, Father. I'm just waiting to see you take a sip of sweet tea. I texted Darby and told her you ordered it, and she doesn't believe me. I need a picture."

Kein laughed so hard tears filled his eyes. Kathy pulled out her phone and set it up. As Kein took a sip, she snapped the photo.

"Ugh—this is terrible stuff," Kein said, grimacing. "Oh no, I can't do that. Could I please have an unsweet tea, Kathy?" He slid the glass back to her.

She laughed and showed him the picture—his face frozen in disgust. She sent it to Darby as they both laughed.

"Tell Darby I said hello and that I am definitely not a sweet tea kind of guy."

On his way home, Kein passed the new age store. It was closed, but he looked through the window at the shelves lined with books on witchcraft and the like. He smiled, knowing he had helped God defeat evil in this place.

Then he saw a figure appear from behind a bookshelf. It moved toward the window—a black, shadowy mass, purposeful and solid. Red eyes stared directly at him. The voice came into his mind, just as God's had.

"You think you've won, priest. You think this is the end. But you see me here—I'm not in the pit where you sent me. I'm stronger than that. I'm not done with you. Now, YOU will be my goal."

The booming voice sent a shudder down Father Kein's back.

"I don't think that's in your best interest, demon," Kein replied calmly.

"I will eat these people from the inside out. They are maggots beneath my feet."

"Well, why don't you tell that to God?" Kein said evenly.

"Go to hell! You are lower than the slop a swine eats!"

Kein brushed a little snow from his coat and looked back at the demon. "You will never win."

The demon rushed the window, stopping inches from Kein's face.

"God is so strong," Kein continued, "even you are afraid to blaspheme His name."

The demon laughed loudly. "Yes, that is true. But you humans—you scream His name in vain. You mock Him daily. We fear Him, but you will fall at our feet for your waste. HA HA HA! WHEN WILL YOU LEARN, PRIEST? YOU LOSE BECAUSE YOU DO NOT FEAR HIM!"

"Well, I guess I'll be on the other side of that battle," Kein said calmly. "And we'll see where the cards fall."

The demon slowly backed away, never breaking its gaze. "You will see how easy it is to sway humans. Pleasure comes in many forms—and we have all of them."

The figure vanished into the shadows. Kein turned and continued home.

Sunday Mass was wonderful. The choir sang, praising Jesus. Eli helped carry the gifts to the altar with his mother. The Bakers sat in the middle of the nave, letting the elderly take the front pews.

After Mass, Kein announced he would be leaving soon. He had received a letter of transfer. Details were still forthcoming, but he would share them when confirmed.

There was sadness—and joy—for the priest who would follow. Redmond had been a wonderful place to spend Christmas. This town showed him that things are not always what they seem and that even at their worst, they can turn around. Above all, he learned that he could stand against darkness and win. His purpose was sacred—sent by God.

Kein returned home and sat at his desk. He picked up the yellow envelope again.

To:

Father Kein Laimend

We hope this letter finds you in good health and continued blessings. We are writing to inform you of a new assignment schedule to be made effective soon.

Father Laimend reassignment schedule as follows:

Relinquish leadership of Saint Augustine's Holy Cathedral, Redmond, North Carolina.
New Assignment: Louisiana, United States of America.
More information to follow.

God's service through you is always appreciated.

Blessed be,
The Catholic

No signature. No specific location.

Kein picked up his phone and dialed.

It rang twice.

“Hello?”

“Rozas,” Kein said, “you’ve got to hear this.”

Afterword

This book grew quieter than I expected.

Where the first story moved quickly and forcefully, this one lingered—watching, waiting, and listening. As I wrote it, I became increasingly aware that not all evil announces itself with violence or spectacle. Sometimes it settles into routine. Sometimes it hides behind reverence. Sometimes it speaks softly enough that we mistake it for peace.

The Silence of Saints is a story about discernment—about learning to recognize when something feels holy, but is not. It asks uncomfortable questions about trust, obedience, and the cost of remaining faithful when clarity is withheld. Father Kein's journey in this book is not marked by triumph, but by endurance and by the quiet realization that faith must often stand without reassurance.

I did not plan where this story would go. Like the first book, I followed it as it unfolded, discovering its weight and direction along the way. What emerged surprised me and, at times, unsettled me. But I believe these are the moments where stories matter most—when they challenge us to sit with silence rather than rush to answers.

Father Kein's work is far from finished. His ministry continues to deepen, and the questions he carries only grow heavier. While this chapter closes quietly, it does not close completely. There is more ahead, and his path will demand even greater trust.

Thank you for walking with him through this season of his calling.

Listen carefully. Not all silence is empty.

This is the second Book in The Unusual Ministries of Father Kein Laimend series.

Book Three is Forthcoming!

Other Books by the Author

Haunted Lake Charles Louisiana: Through the eyes of a Lead Paranormal Investigator

The Unusual Ministries of Father Kein Laimend: The First Real Assignment

About the Author

Marcus has had a passion for writing for as long as he can remember—from early journal entries to short stories, even earning awards for his work during his school years. Like many of his creative pursuits, such as dancing, writing is something he approaches wholeheartedly, often immersing himself completely and forming deep connections with the characters as they come to life on the page.

An author, filmmaker, and storyteller, Marcus's work explores the intersection of faith, mystery, and the unexplained. His writing blends atmospheric suspense with spiritual depth, inviting readers into worlds where belief is tested, courage is revealed, and unseen forces challenge what we think we know. His first book, *Haunted Lake Charles, Louisiana: Through the Eyes of a Lead Paranormal Investigator*, draws from his experience investigating the paranormal and examining how faith intersects with the unknown. His second book, *The Unusual Ministries of Father Kein Laimend: The First Real Assignment*, marked the beginning of a faith-driven fictional series exploring spiritual warfare, obedience, and sacrifice.

Marcus has been featured on *Louisiana's Playground*, where he discussed paranormal investigations and the role of faith in everyday life. He also holds credits in film and television as a director, producer, and actor and is the creator of the paranormal investigation Docuseries *Spirit Guides*, demonstrating a creative versatility across multiple mediums.

At the heart of his work is a belief he holds close: spend time each day talking to God—but more importantly, spend time each day listening. He believes God has a plan for everyone and that some of the most powerful moments come when we are quiet enough to hear it.

www.ingramcontent.com/pod-product-compliance
Lightning Source LLC
LaVergne TN
LVHW090526110826
845146LV00003B/995
9798994560822